About the author

Tony Flannagan was born in Portsmouth.

In 2017, his debut children's novel *The Most Curious Case of the Runaway Spoon* was published by Pegasus Elliott Mackenzie Publishers.

Tony lives in Hampshire with his wife, children and their golden retriever, Bertie.

MOZZARELLA BELLA AND THE ENGLISH FELLA

Also, by Tony Flannagan

The Most Curious Case of the Runaway Spoon

Tony Flannagan

MOZZARELLA BELLA AND THE ENGLISH FELLA

Vanguard Press

VANGUARD PAPERBACK

© Copyright 2019
Tony Flannagan
Cover design by Dominic Campbell

A CIP catalogue record for this title is
available from the British Library.

ISBN 978 1 784655 38 9

Vanguard Press is an imprint of
Pegasus Elliot MacKenzie Publishers Ltd.
www.pegasuspublishers.com

First Published in 2019

Vanguard Press
Sheraton House Castle Park
Cambridge England

Printed & Bound in Great Britain

Dedication

To Lucas, Aden and Abby…
who knew the real Bella.

"Wherever we may be, there will be Rome."
Giuseppe Garibaldi

Carpe Diem

O MISTRESS mine, where are you roaming?
O stay and hear! your true-love's coming
That can sing both high and low;
Trip no further, pretty sweeting,
Journey's end in lovers' meeting –
Every wise man's son doth know.

What is love? 'tis not hereafter;
Present mirth hath present laughter;
What's to come is still unsure:
In delay there lies no plenty, –
Then come kiss me, Sweet-and-twenty,
Youth's a stuff will not endure.

William Shakespeare

Day 1

St Peter's Basilica – *Il Duomo*

I

The bundle of black rags got up slowly. A trembling hand reached out and held onto the step for balance as the decrepit figure struggled to her feet.

'Get away with you, old woman, sitting there in your stinking rags, feeding the wretched cats. Go on, away with you, or I'll have you in the cells!' Police Chief Romano swung a booted foot at the retreating figure. The kick was deliberately wide of its mark, for even Romano accepted that to kick the Gattara would actually make him look like a brute. He was, by his own admission, a very real brute. In fact, he was a brute of the highest order, and this was something of which he was immensely proud. But the last thing he needed was any do-gooding tourist filing a complaint with the Comandante Generale. So, Romano contented himself with miming a penalty kick: he shuffled backwards, scraped at the cobbled street with his immaculately polished black boots, ran forward with great determination, his tongue lolling comically from side-to-side, and kicked at the spot the Gattara had recently vacated.

Romano turned in mock celebration as the Gattara hobbled away.

Goal!

Phew!

Romano took a handkerchief from his trouser pocket and dusted at his sleeves. Then, he bent down and wiped the toecaps of his boots. Satisfied that he had buffed them back to their original mirror-shine, Romano stood back up, pushed his white cap back off his forehead and mopped at his sweating brow. It was hot this morning. Not a cloud in the azure sky above the Eternal City.

'Okay, folks, the show is over. And please be warned: do *not*, under any circumstances, feed the cats!' Romano placed his hands behind his back and puffed out his chest. 'It is an offence decreed by the City Council of Rome to feed any of the stray cats that pollute the city.' Romano pointed to a notice stuck to the window of a boarded-up pizzeria. 'Some people do not listen, and they pay the price. But you must understand – oh, you really must please understand – that these feral vermin are not like your pet pussies in old London town, and they are not like *die katzen* in Berlin or *les chats* in gay Paris. No, sir; and no, madam; there are no cutie-pie-sweet-little-kitties here. The *gatti*, I mean the cats, are street vermin, and it is forbidden to feed them.'

The tourists giggled, nervously. Someone in the crowd, for some unexplained reason, clapped and others hesitantly joined in. Others remained silent or nudged each other and pulled faces.

What was it with this ugly policeman?

Are we supposed to clap?

Where has the guide gotten to?

I hope we haven't paid for this sideshow!

Romano was ugly. He knew this. He was an ugly brute in looks, thoughts and deeds. He didn't have one, single redeeming feature, and he did not care a fig. Romano held up an appreciative hand. He had his audience captive. 'So please, please, do *not* feed the cats – and that includes you, young man…' Romano looked directly at the boy wearing a *Let's Go Mets* t-shirt.

Romano took one slow, giant step closer to the boy.

The boy recoiled and hid behind his mother's skirt.

Romano stepped back, holding his hands to his chest in mock reproach. The crowd murmured. There was something about the policeman that made you not want to trust him one little bit, which also meant you couldn't take your eyes off him for a single moment. Romano was an expert in playing the part of the pantomime villain. 'Please do not be like this Gattara, this old cat woman, who feeds the feline parasites and brings disease upon the Eternal City.' Romano turned around and shouted, 'Go on, old cat lady – away with you!' And Romano waved his arms wildly to shoo the Gattara on her way.

The crowd fell silent.

The Gattara cast an angry, backward glance at Romano and offered up a mute curse to the cloudless sky from beneath her headscarf. But Romano was now too preoccupied with his performance to take any notice of what the old woman might have had to say. Instead, he concentrated his attention on aiming his shiny police boots at the coterie of stringy cats who skipped after the Gattara as she disappeared down a side street. 'Go on, the lot of you, get out of here!'

A brown tortoiseshell cat sat on the step vacated by the old woman, eating a slice of pizza. Bella looked up, raised her chin, and blinked slowly at Romano.

'Hello, I don't recognise you. Why not? I know all the cats in this district, so you must be new around here, eh? Please be warned, little kitty-cat, that if I ever see you around here again scrounging pizza…' Without warning, Romano picked up a loose cobble from the street and threw it at Bella. For a big man he moved with surprising speed, and she only just managed to leap out of harm's way. Romano gave chase as Bella sprinted down the side street in pursuit of the Gattara and safety. Romano stopped abruptly, puffing out his cheeks as he held on to the pole of a street sign to steady himself while he caught his breath. 'Now, folks,' he panted, 'let's all be moving on now. This show is most definitely over.'

The tourists mumbled to themselves:

Did you see that?

I'm sure that cat just stared him out.

What a bully that policeman is!

Mind you, the old woman isn't helping matters by feeding them…

Someone spotted the tour guide's red umbrella in the distance, and the group of tourists took the cue to follow-their-leader and shuffled along the cobbled street.

A girl came out of a nearby restaurant to collect cups and plates from the empty tables. She moved hurriedly and with determination.

'Maria?'

The girl ignored the policeman and carried on fetching the crockery.

'Maria… Thank you, I now have your attention. Please, tell your father that if I catch him leaving titbits of food out for the cats again, I will have his restaurant licence revoked, do you hear me? I know it was Toni who fed that brown tortoiseshell cat that was sat over there eating pizza. Yes? A slice of your not-so-famous margherita pizza all the way from the not-so-bella Napoli,' mocked Romano.

The girl did not look up. She nodded with tight lips and continued about her work.

Charlie stopped sketching. He watched the girl sweep a loose strand of hair behind her ear and then hurriedly disappear back inside the restaurant. He looked up at the sign: *La Margherita*. Hardly original for a pizzeria; and what a life – waiting on awful tourists all day… Mind you, it wouldn't be so bad if those same awful tourists bought his pictures. But they never did. They just smiled politely and walked on by, saving their money to buy the soulless, computer-generated images from the con-artists in Piazza Navona. How on earth was he going to get the money to enter the end-of-course art exhibition that was only a week away?

'Have you got a street licence, boy?'

Charlie looked up from beneath his fringe. 'I'm sorry. No speak Italian. I'm an English person, from England.' Charlie pointed dumbly at himself. 'English person,' he repeated, slowly.

Romano stood over Charlie, who was sat on the cobbles surrounded by his watercolours and sketches. He pointed to his own chest and spoke in heavily accented English: '*P-o-l-i-c-e-man*… Now, if you haven't gotta-the-licence to sell this-a-rubbish that you litter the pavement with, I'll stick you in-a-the cell with the old cat lady!'

Charlie held up his plastic photo ID. As a student of the *Accademia Delle Belle Arti di Roma* he was entitled to a street artist's licence for the length of his college stay.

Romano grabbed at the lanyard and pulled Charlie up from the pavement. '*Studente*!' Romano hollered, reverting back to his native Italian. 'Another-a-lazy good-for-nothing student scrounging on the streets of Rome, just like all those feral cats!'

Charlie spoke in his best Italian: 'Woah! Signor, please. I'm not lazy. Good for nothing, maybe... But definitely not lazy, if you please.'

Romano stepped back. He was a bit put out and confused by Charlie speaking to him in Italian, and he stared hard at the floppy-haired boy. A sixth sense made Romano let go his grip and he turned around with a broad smile fixed on his huge face.

All of a sudden, Romano was speaking in fluent German to the blonde-haired couple who were stood watching. 'Illegal street trader,' he said. 'Vermin, all over the place... Now, if I may...' Without being asked, Romano offered the bemused couple directions to a very good restaurant in Piazza del Paradiso.

It was no problem at all. Here, let me show you; my sister runs this delightful little place. Come. Bitte...

Charlie gathered up his pictures. He looked across the street. The girl was back outside the restaurant, talking to a heavily moustached man who was sat at a shaded table next to the door.

Charlie smiled at the girl. He was almost certain he had seen her before... at the *Accademia*? Yes! She was the one with *the* most incredible blue eyes. Even from across the street, Charlie could see they were as blue as sapphires.

Blue as sapphires – what was he thinking?

As if able to read his thoughts, the girl looked up and laughed. Charlie watched her nervously tuck another loose strand of hair behind her ear. The girl blushed, and again reached up to her hair with her left hand, while her right remained tucked out of sight in the pocket of her apron.

Sapphires – whatever would he think of next? Charlie needed a coffee.

'Are these your pictures? I say, excuse me – did you draw these pictures?' said a woman with an American accent.

Charlie shook his gaze away from the girl and turned to a woman wearing a huge hat that flopped about her face as she spoke.

The woman pointed.

Charlie nodded. 'Yes. They are all my own original work.'

'They're very nice. Are you British?'

Charlie nodded.

'I thought so. Do you know the Hampson-Smiths of Acton, in London?'

Charlie shook his head. 'No, I'm afraid I don't… Should I know them?'

'Not really. That's a shame, but they're very nice – your pictures, not the Hampson-Smiths. But they, too, are very nice – the Hampson-Smiths that is,' said the woman. 'Now come on, AJ, we have to go; your father is waiting…' The woman tugged at the hand of the little boy wearing a *Let's Go Mets* t-shirt, dragging him away from Charlie's collection of sketches and towards the Piazza Navona.

II

Another day in Rome - except, there is no such thing as *just another day* when you're in Rome. This much I have learned since I arrived here. And so, I sang to myself as I crossed the street:

I'm walking pretty
Through the streets of the Eternal City
Wherever I roam, every street's my home
When I'm roaming in Rome

'Well, look who it is: the Mozzarella Bella... and where have you been roaming this fine morning? You come for your breakfast, eh? You want the pizza?'

Meet Toni-Macaroni, owner of my favourite restaurant: *La Margherita*. I like Toni-Macaroni; he looks after me. He says it's because we are both from Naples. Don't ask me how he knows this; it's just something that we Neapolitans know, I suppose. And Toni-Macaroni always says the same thing, every morning. But I'm not complaining, because Toni-Macaroni serves up the best breakfast in all of Rome.

'Meow-meow-meow… Hey, Amerigo, if I didn't know better, I would swear that the Mozzarella Bella was talking to me.'

But I am talking to you, Toni. You may come from Naples and have the Neapolitan sixth sense, but you sure as heck don't understand cat-talk.

'Meow-meow… But just as long as she hasn't brought her friends along today, because they all have very bad manners, Toni, and there are so many of them. I swear that good-for-nothing fascist Romano will have your licence if you keep feeding them.'

Now, this Amerigo fella, he was always at the bar, morning, noon and *notte*. I never saw him move from his table by the door, always reading the newspaper, drinking coffee, moaning about the government and life in general. I mean, get a life, old man.

'Mozzarella Bella… Whoever heard of a cat eating pizza?' grumbled Amerigo.

Really, the ignorance of some people - believe it or not, I like pizza. And that is why Toni-Macaroni calls me the Mozzarella Bella. I think it started as a joke, but the name stuck. And we have this same conversation *every* day. But this is Italy, and that is what we do: talk and talk, and then we talk some more about the same things *every* day. If we're not talking about food, we're talking about

25

life; if we're not talking about life, we're talking about food. And if we are not talking, we eat and sleep, or watch football. That's the way it is. So, the Mozzarella Bella started to call her benefactor 'Toni-Macaroni'. And it rhymes, too. Only, he doesn't know that I call him Toni-Macaroni; the only ones who know this are me and my friends: Adriana, Franco and Bobby. Besides, as I said earlier, Toni-Macaroni doesn't talk cat. Even the Neapolitan sixth sense can't get over this little language barrier. But here is the real meal deal: my friends and I keep the rats away from the restaurant and Toni-Macaroni keeps us in food. Which all sounds pretty straightforward, right? And, for the most part, it is a simple enough arrangement. But have you seen how many bars and restaurants there are in Rome? Hundreds and thousands of them; I mean, how else would all the tourists get fed? But with all the food places comes a lot of left-over food, and with all the left-over food? You got it: with the left-over food you get the rats! And that is where we cats come in. They don't call us the Lions of Rome for nothing, you know.

Now, you would think with all of these bars and restaurants in Rome there would be more than enough work for us cats to busy ourselves with in and around the Eternal City. But you'd be wrong, quite wrong. Because while there may be hundreds and thousands of eating places and hundreds and thousands of rats, there are millions and millions of us cats. And that means there is plenty of competition. Especially around the piazzas, where the choicest bars and restaurants attract the wealthier tourists. So, that is why people like Toni-Macaroni want their places free of rats, and they are willing to pay us handsomely to ensure that the rodents are kept in check. But, as I said, the *quid pro quo* arrangement brings a lot of competition and a heck of a lot of rivalry, and it isn't always healthy.

You see, cats tend to be very territorial. For example, take Adriana and Franco. They tend to work two of Rome's most famous spots, the Piazza Navona and the Piazza della Rotonda; while Bobby thinks he's an *Americano* and hangs around the larger hotels. And this all works out fine if you stick to your own district. It's when you stray off-patch that the troubles ensue. I tend to be a bit of a wanderer. I guess you could say I am the 'PR' side of our little outfit. Adriana and Franco do the ratting, while I do the chatting. You see, we all have our specialties, and mine is the natural-born Neapolitan ability to charm.

But now there is an added problem. A new by-law brought in by this Romano character, who I've somehow managed to avoid up to now. According to this new by-law, the restaurants, bars and pizzerias are not supposed to feed us. Apparently, it is us cats that are the *real* vermin and a much bigger problem than the rats. So, if any restaurant or bar gets caught feeding the cats, then they run the risk of being closed down. As I said, this piece of legislation was the work of Romano, and the worst thing about him is that he exclusively works in our district.

'Now, remember to share your spoils with your friends, even though they have the very bad manners. There's a little salami, and the ham, some pepperoni, and, of course, your very special favourite – a little cheese and tomato pizza for the Mozzarella Bella from Napoli. Ha-ha! Say, Amerigo, I swear to you this cat can talk.'

Amerigo looked up from his newspaper. 'How can you say that cat can talk? And why do you say it comes from Naples? How can you tell? It's just a cat. There are thousands of them in this district alone. They all look the same to me.'

'Not like this one, Amerigo. She's smart. A real street cat. A Neapolitan cat.'

'Are you saying the Roman cats are stupid, Toni? If that's the case, I'll take my custom elsewhere.' Amerigo slurped cappuccino froth all over his whiskers. I watched as he licked at his lips and moustache. He must have been a cat in a previous life – sitting around all day, just watching, eating and drinking, licking at his whiskers.

'Calm yourself, Amerigo. I'm sure there are many street-wise cats in Rome. It's just that the Mozzarella Bella has got this look about her. Now, where is that daughter of mine? Maria!'

'How do you put up with that guy?' says Adriana, pulling a face.

'Yeah, how do you put up with the Toni-Ravioli,' says Franco.

'Macaroni!' corrects Bobby.

'Whatever. Macaroni, Ravioli, Bangers-and-Mash-and-Minestrone...,' laughs Franco.

'*Gatti*, please!' I say. 'It's easy to humour Toni-Macaroni. Come on, he keeps his side of the bargain and we keep ours. It's that simple. Now, come, fellow *gatti* – enjoy the feast.'

We tuck into the breakfast. There is enough to feed a whole army.

'Say, you *gatti* aren't going to keep all that food to yourselves, surely?'

I look up to see the handsome face of Marco Del Vecchio, the most elegant and not-so-eligible tomcat in the whole of the district.

'*Buongiorno*, Marco,' I say.

'*Ciao*, Bella, how's it going this fine morning? I could ask that question, but what is the point?

Because I see that everything is fine and sugar-dandy with you guys. Ain't that right, *gatti*?'

'You could say that, Marco,' coos Adriana, who always acts like a smitten-kitten when Marco is around. Silly Adriana, whatever would Angelina think?

'I could say that, I would, and I did. Everything is just fine and sugar-dandy.' Marco runs a paw over his whiskers. He is a chocolate brown colour with white socks, and he always keeps himself immaculately groomed.

'Would you like to join us?' I say.

Franco regards me with a look that says: *Well, that's just fantastico!* Franco is the greediest cat in all of Rome. He was once the greediest cat in Paris, until one day he jumped on a train at the Gare de Lyon and ended up at Roma Termini.

'Oh, yes; there is plenty here for you and *all* your friends,' says Adriana, fluttering her long eyelashes.

At this, Franco takes a great mouthful of pizza and pads over to the other side of the street.

'I say, Frenchman, you have very bad manners,' shouts Marco.

Franco doesn't look up from his food. He keeps his head down and munches.

'Very bad manners indeed; but I forgive him, for he is one of the best "ratters" in Rome and such prowess affords me and my friends to partake of such a fine breakfast.'

Franco hears Marco. He never misses a compliment, but he doesn't respond and simply shrugs and carries on eating. Franco doesn't mean to be rude, nor does he have bad manners. But he is moody. You see, as Marco says, Franco is the greatest ratter in Rome, and his skill allows him to get away with things other cats would be too scared to contemplate. Besides, Franco is hopelessly in love with Adriana, but has never plucked up the courage to tell her. So, when Marco Del Vecchio and his gang of smooth-talkers are around, Franco tends to get the sulks and grumps off. Apparently, that is why he jumped on that train in Paris: he had fallen in love with a girl in Montmartre, but she was too much in love with the *ooh-la-la*, which wasn't to Franco's liking.

'Oh, Marco…'

'Yes, Adriana?'

'How is Angelina?'

Give Adriana her due, she has some nerve.

'Oh, Angelina is good, I suppose. I haven't seen her around lately.' Marco shakes his head and eats.

Hasn't seen her around? Who is Marco trying to fool? Angelina Belletti is the prettiest cat in all of Rome. It is rumoured that she was once offered a part in a movie but turned it down in order to stay on the streets with Marco. He got mad at her because he said they could have done with the money. But I ask you, what good is money to a cat?

'Well, if you ever need any company, all you've got to do is ask.'

'Ah, Adriana, that is a very kind and considerate offer, but I have a pretty full diary at the moment. However, if I get some spare time... well, you never know, I'll be sure to look you up.'

'I'll be waiting.'

What a flirt! If Angelina ever found out about this, Adriana would be in such *big* trouble. Angelina is as fierce as she is pretty, and if anybody ever messed about with Marco, well, that would not be quite so pretty.

While Marco eats his breakfast, his gang stands about the street on lookout.

'Are your boys not hungry?' I say.

Marco does not look up from his salami. 'Nah, they probably already ate. Besides, they're on business.'

Here we go again: *Business.*

'And what business would that be?'

'You know, Bella, looking after things. Making sure that everything around here is all right, just fine and sugar-dandy. You gotta keep the streets safe; right, Bella?' And with that, Marco fixes me with *that* smile.

Now, that smile could either send a chill through an enemy or melt a girl's heart, and its quality was not entirely lost on me. So, I look back to the single slice of pizza that remained, in order to divert my eyes from Marco's gaze. I know that in order to keep the streets safe Marco, and others like him, have to go about their business. And it works like this: Marco and his boys keep to the streets around this district, and the other gangs keep to those parts of the city that belong to them. This so-called *business* is pretty much about keeping your streets safe for you and your gang. If another gang comes onto your patch – well, that means *business* of a different kind. And all this *business* is the reason I left Naples, because that is not the life for me. No, signor and signore; I just like to roam when I'm in Rome; but these cats in the Eternal City are so territorial and it causes no end of problems.

'Boss, we gotta go,' shouts one of the lookouts.

'Okay, Gino.' Marco turns to walk away. 'See you around, Bella. Finish up your mozzarella. Hey, *Mozzarella Bella*! I like it. That's what I'll call you from now on. It's a good name, and with you coming from Naples, it sort of fits.'

'Somebody else already does call her the Mozzarella Bella.' Franco has finished eating and walks back over, probably because he sees that

Marco and his gang are getting ready to leave and he wants to see if there is any food left.

'And who is this person who dares to call her the Mozzarella Bella?' quizzes Marco.

'Wouldn't you like to know who calls her the Mozzarella Bella,' says Franco.

Hey guys. What do they mean: *her*? *Hello, I'm here!* But it's fairly clear that Marco and Franco are in a little tomcat world of their own.

'Why, it's Toni-Macaroni who calls her the Mozzarella Bella.'

'And who is this Toni-Macaroni? He's not a cat I'm familiar with.'

'And I thought you knew everybody and everything that went on in these streets. Perhaps you need new blood in your gang.'

Somebody is pushing their luck.

Marco walks right up and stands nose-to-nose with Franco. 'Where does this Toni-Macaroni do his business?'

'Where, indeed; wouldn't you like to know?'

'I would indeed.'

'Well, it's right here and right now – in this street, right under your nose...'

And I'm thinking: *Franco – NO!*

'You're telling me this Toni-Macaroni guy does his business in this very street? In *my* district...' Marco is bristling.

'In *your* district, Marco... Right under *your* nose.'

'Boss, Luca Luigi and his gang – they're at the Pantheon!'

One of the lookouts has come running over.

'I gotta go. But, Franco, you and me, we need to talk.'

Adriana swoons. She loves all this tough-guy nonsense.

Franco tries to make a grab for the last slice of pizza.

He has very bad manners, but I am too quick for him and I trot across the street to the Gattara, who is sat on a step feeding some of the younger cats with little treats that she keeps in her pockets. There's something about the Gattara and the way she keeps a lookout in this particular street; it's as if she's waiting for something. I don't know; just call it the Neapolitan sixth sense.

As I said, there's no such thing as just another day in Rome.

III

Charlie woke up and stared at the cracks in the ceiling and looked at the peeling walls. He listened to the noise coming in through the open balcony doors and smiled. The morning chorus was reaching its crescendo, a symphony of chatter, clatter and horns.

Beep!

Beep!

Beep!

That would be Nico calling for Leonora, who lived in the next apartment block. The same three beeps of the Lambretta horn every morning. Monday through to Friday, Nico would give Leonora a lift to college; on Saturday he would take her to acting lessons, and on a Sunday, he would collect her for church. Charlie got up, ruffled his hair, checked it was a passable mess in the wardrobe mirror and padded out to the balcony.

Nico looked up and pointed to his watch.

Charlie tapped his wrist, rolled his eyes and held up his hands.

Nico shook his head.

Charlie shrugged his shoulders and laughed.

They went through this same ritual every day. It was only 8 o'clock. Back home in England, Charlie would have still been asleep in bed. He wouldn't have got up for college until his mother had called him at least a dozen times. Since arriving in Rome his body clock had adjusted naturally to the early starts. Besides, he didn't want to miss a single minute of this crazy city. Charlie looked out across the Piazza della Rotunda. It was going to be another hot day. The sun's golden rays reflected off the dome of the Pantheon and painted the piazza a misty yellow. The hooves of the horses clattered on the cobbles as the carts took their place in line; the drivers jumped down and stood about talking, gesticulating, smoking cigarettes and drinking espressos. Awnings were unfurled, tables wiped, and chairs scraped into place outside the bars and restaurants. The first walking train of tourists, bleary-eyed and heavy-footed, snaked under Charlie's balcony. He loved this apartment and he loved the piazza; the rent had been paid up front and, despite the fact that he was just about out of money, he still had nearly a fortnight to enjoy his room with a view.

'Charlie!' Leonora looked up and waved.

Charlie smiled and stuck up a thumb.

Nico hit Charlie with a hard stare and nodded, the friendly banter gone until tomorrow morning at least.

Charlie watched as Nico handed Leonora her helmet. Leonora kissed Nico on both cheeks in the manner that Italians always greeted each other, something that the not-so-tactile Charlie had taken a little while to get used to, because if a girl kissed you back in England it meant *something*. Not in Rome, as the old song said: *a kiss is just a kiss* – no different to just saying 'hello'; and you must remember this, I mean even the boys kissed each other, something that Charlie was still very uncomfortable with, preferring to fist-bump if he could get a greeting in first. *If only Nico had the courage to ask Leonora out*, thought Charlie. Nico had been fetching and carrying Leonora for nearly two years now. In one unguarded moment, Nico had told Charlie that he was hopelessly in love with Leonora but didn't want to ask her out because if she said 'no', it would break his heart, and if they did go out with each other, and then split up, he wouldn't be able to pick her up again, and that would be the worst thing ever. Charlie shook his head as Nico gunned the Lambretta engine and weaved his scooter through the line of tourists.

Hey!

Where're you going, buddy?

Jeez! Did you see that!
The guy's a maniac!
And what's with all these cats…?

A boy in a *Let's Go Mets* t-shirt looked up at Charlie.

Charlie waved.

The boy snatched at the hand of a woman wearing a big floppy hat and was silently admonished for the sudden movement that caused her to topple on her heels and break her stride.

Charlie stretched. It was time to collect his sketches and paintings and walk over to Via della Verita – the Street of Truth. And the real truth of the matter was that Charlie was running out of money fast. His mother had told him that she was not going to send him over any more once the course had ended. More like Roger wasn't going to let her send any more money. *You would have thought that he should have been glad to be rid of me for a few weeks*, thought Charlie. At this rate, he wasn't going to have enough money to get through the last week at the *Accademia* and pay his exhibition entry fee. Perhaps, today, he would sell a few pictures. Perhaps, the girl from *La Margherita* restaurant would walk across the street, look at him with those magnificent blue eyes and invite him over for a coffee. Charlie laughed. What had his advice been to Nico? *Just tell her*. For the first time in his young life, Charlie thought that he might be in love, but he didn't know if it was with the girl or Rome. And he was sure that he had seen her at the *Accademia*, but she didn't hang out with Leonora and any of her friends which seemed strange. Charlie stretched and yawned.

Another day in Rome.

IV

Maria stood at her bedroom window looking down into the shady street below. Amerigo was already sat at his regular table, reading the newspaper. You could set your watch by the comings and goings in Via della Verita. In two days, it would be the anniversary of Mamma's death. One whole year. It still felt as though things would never be anything like the same again. Time had not been a great healer, especially for Papa. Maria turned as the alarm clock rang out in his room. It would continue to ring until Maria walked across the landing and into his room to switch it off. It wasn't that his ears were failing him; he just didn't want to hear the sound of the alarm clock heralding another day.

Another day in Rome without Mamma.

Maria slipped the black lace glove, which she'd adapted by cutting off the fingers, on her right wrist and grabbed her apron from the bed. She had tidied her room and packed her college bag, being careful to rearrange the pyramid of text books she didn't need to take with her today on top of the trunk that sat on the floor at the foot of her bed. Maria walked over to Papa's room, switched the alarm off and shook his shoulder.

'What? Is it time to get up already?' yawned Papa.

'Yes, Papa.'

Maria walked quietly out of the room and made her way downstairs to the restaurant. She looked at frames with the media cuttings and pictures of Mamma from the movies that still adorned the restaurant walls. It was time for the morning routine to begin in earnest.

Another day in Rome.

V

Romano looked at his reflection in the mirror. It was true to say that he had never been a handsome man; even as a boy he knew his looks were never going to be the thing that drew people to him. That was why he had cultivated the image of the strong, no-nonsense policeman. Now, people looked up to him. Now, they noticed him. Nobody could ignore Police Chief Romano.

As a boy, Romano had been shy. His parents thought he was a mute, and so his sister Paola would talk for him.

His mother would moan, 'What is wrong with you, Luigi, why have you not finished your spaghetti?'

His sister would reply, 'Luigi is not hungry, mamma. He wants to go to the cinema to watch films.'

His father would say, 'That boy lives in a fantasy world.'

'But it's good to have dreams, papa.' Paola knew all about her brother's love of the cinema and his desire to be a famous actor or producer so he could meet the beautiful Valeria Viola, the famous actress from Naples.

'What good are dreams if he won't tell anyone what is going on in his head?' And at this point his mother would begin to cry.

Paola would say, 'Don't cry, mamma. Luigi will come back as soon as the film has finished.'

His father would reach across the table and pat Romano's face. 'You're a good boy, Luigi. Here, take some money and go watch your film. One day, when you are working with Federico Fellini, you can buy your sister her own *ristorante* and mamma and I can retire to the mountains. But first you need to speak up for yourself!'

Romano's parents had never got to retire to the mountains. They had died indebted to the money-lenders and fixers who controlled Rome's back-street economy. Romano and his sister had to find work. Paola had been studying to be a vet: she was forever bringing home sick and wounded cats, much to the horror of their parents, who thought the pathetic animals carried all manner of diseases. Romano resented the attention that his sister gave to the wretched creatures. Paola would wash, clean and fix the cats, before sending them back out into the street or taking them to the cat ladies at the Torre Argentina Sanctuary. Paola had a gift. But the family was poor, and when their parents died so did any dreams of Paola getting a college education. There would be no veterinary practice for Paola and no film school for Romano. It was the life of a waitress for her and that of a plate-washer for him. But at least he had finally got to meet the beautiful Valeria Viola – his beloved '*Vivi*' – when he started work at *La Margherita* in Via della Verita. Then, he had left the restaurant to join the police and Luigi Romano finally found his voice.

Romano dragged the razor blade across the stubble of his beard. He could shave ten times a day, but his beard would still show through blue and bristly, a permanent dark shadow masking his features. Romano blotted his face with the dirty towel, stood up straight and buttoned up his policeman's tunic. He looked from his reflection in the mirror to the film poster that hung next to the bathroom sink. True love, that's what it was. Romano's love for Valeria Viola would never diminish. It would soon be a year since her death. The love he felt for her was stronger than ever, as was the disgust that he felt for her good-for-nothing husband, Toni. The same was true of the daughter, Maria. Why, if Valeria had married Romano, their children would have been perfect. Maria was the offspring of a weak man and that was the reason she had her disability. As far as Romano was concerned a weak and pathetic man begets deformed children, and Toni was the weakest and most pathetic man he had ever known. Romano threw his razor into the dirty water. It made him angry to think of everything that had happened and the circumstances of Valeria's death. Now, he would never get to be with *his* beloved *'Vivi'*. Today would be as empty as yesterday. Tomorrow, Romano's sense of loss and anger would remain just as strong. Today would be another painful day for Romano, although nobody would see or ever be able to guess at the hurt within. Today…

Another day in Rome.

Day 2

A room with a view…

VI

Charlie walked into the refectory. Heads turned. They always did when Charlie walked into a room. Charlie nodded, fist-bumped the boys and stopped to exchange kisses with the girls, and some of the boys. It may only have been three weeks since he had enrolled at the *Accademia*, but he already felt at home in Rome. He didn't mind all the attention and being called: *English*. Maybe it was because he didn't have to put up a front here. Not like back home, where everybody was consumed with everything and nothing. He could hear all the college mums now: *Simon has got an internship in the City… Jeremy has been selected for the Colts… Charlotte got straight A-Star grades in all her subjects and we're thinking maybe Cardiff because they had an excellent grading in the Times…* Charlie had been accepted for a one-month summer course at the *Accademia Delle Belle Arti di Roma* after completing his A-levels. During his time at sixth-form, he'd increasingly felt like an outsider and no longer shared the interests and aspirations of his childhood friends; but here, in Rome, he felt like he truly belonged. The people here just got on with living life. Nobody judged him. The language barrier helped, although he could speak passable Italian from his A-Level studies he couldn't understand the vast majority of what people were saying, which meant he didn't have to listen to them talking nonsense. For the first time in his young adult life, Charlie felt that he could relax and be himself.

And there she was.

Charlie extricated himself from Nico's embrace.

The girl was reading.

Charlie walked boldly towards her table.

She was consumed with the large book that lay open in front of her, and as he approached, she looked up. Charlie felt his step falter and his heart stop.

'Hello.' The girl spoke in English.

Charlie swallowed hard, desperately trying to find his voice.

The girl closed the book on her right hand and looked at him inquisitively.

'You're the girl from the restaurant in Via della Verita,' blurted Charlie.

The girl smiled. 'You mean the pizzeria?'

'I take it that you work at the *pizzeria* to help pay for your education. I'm looking for a job myself at the moment. I don't seem to be able to sell enough

pictures to pay for the end-of-course exhibition…'
What was he talking about? *Shut up, Charlie!* 'I see
you outside the restaurant most mornings.'

'What are you? An English spy… or the Mr
Sherlock Holmes, perhaps?'

Charlie put his hands behind his back. 'Now,
signorina, let me see. Your name is... Wait, I know
it – Maria!'

The girl looked suitably impressed. 'You have
quite a gift.'

Charlie bowed and sat down at the table.
'Elementary, my dear, Maria.'

Maria pulled a face as if to indicate that she had
no idea what Charlie was talking about.

'It's what Sherlock Holmes used to say to
Watson...'

Maria shook her head.

'Sorry, bad joke.'

'No, wait. I see…' The girl spoke to herself in
Italian and considered carefully: *Elementare, mio
caro Watson.* 'No, I think it was a good joke,
Charlie.'

Charlie rocked back on his chair. 'Wait, how do
you know my name?'

Maria blushed. 'Everybody knows you as the
English… I mean, you are Charlie from England,
right? Your reputation goes before you.'

'All good, I hope.'

'No, I'm afraid it's not good - definitely all bad.'

Charlie sat back in his chair and opened his arms wide. *What?*

'Now it's my turn to make the joke.'

Charlie looked closely at Maria. No wonder he had checked his stride and lost his voice. It was her eyes. The sea and the sky were no match for them. But they were totally wrong. Italian girl checklist: brown hair – tick; tawny skin – tick; skinny arms – got it; brown eyes… but Maria's eyes were *blue*, and Charlie couldn't help but stare at them. 'How do you do, Maria.' Charlie shook himself back to the present and extended his right hand.

Maria considered. 'How very English.' She put down her pencil and held out her left hand.

'Boy Scouts handshake?' Charlie ventured.

'Boy Scouts? What is this?'

'Left-handed. Apparently, the Ashanti chiefs told Lord Baden-Powell that only truly brave warriors shook with their left hand.

It was Maria's turn to mouth: *What?*

'The reason being, that the warriors held their shields in the left hand, their weaker hand, and to put down the shield was to show true strength and respect… which assumes that the warrior was right-handed. Um, I don't know what the left-handed warriors did. I presume they got killed. It's all to do with the Boer War, I think. All very strange really; and talking of *bores...*' The latter was more of an aside to himself. *What was he going on about!*

Maria shook her head and laughed. 'Charlie, I have no idea what you're talking about!'

What was wrong with him? He was a bumbling wreck and babbling on like a right proper... *Charlie*, *pull it together*! He rolled his eyes and extended his left hand.

The touch of Maria's hand was electric. It was as if a thousand tiny lightning bolts had gone off in his fingers. Charlie stared at the long, slender fingers that he held in his grasp.

'Charlie... Hello, Charlie?'

'Yes? Sorry, what?'

'Can I have my hand back, please?'

Charlie was so consumed with his thoughts that he had inadvertently held on tightly to Maria's hand. What was it about this girl? He caught himself staring again, this time at her smiling, quizzical face. It was definitely the eyes. *Okay, recovery time.* 'And I see that you play a musical instrument. The violin, perhaps?'

Maria's face reddened and her eyes turned to grey.

'No, wait - the piano?'

'Bad joke, Charlie.' Maria snatched back her hand and returned to her reading.

Charlie was dumbstruck. What had happened? He looked at Maria: she had gone very red. *Why was she cross? Had he upset her? What had he said that was so wrong?* Charlie tried to catch her eye and went to speak.

Maria didn't look up from her book. 'Goodbye, Charlie.'

'Hello, Charlie! Where have you been?' It was Leonora. She came sauntering across the refectory with Patricia. The two friends were inseparable. 'Come this way, Charlie,' she said, taking hold of Charlie's arm and dragging him out of the chair. As they walked away, Leonora whispered, 'Anyway, why are you talking to the pirate?'

Patricia took hold of Charlie by his other arm. 'Yes, the one-armed bandit – why are you sitting with her?'

What were they talking about? Girls, they could be so bitchy. I mean, just because Maria was left-handed - he presumed she was left-handed - how else could you explain the boy-scout handshake? But there was no need to speak about her like that. Leonora and Patricia were probably just jealous because he was speaking to her, and that's why Maria's mood had changed so quickly – maybe she saw the two girls coming and they didn't get on? Charlie looked back over his shoulder. Maria had packed up her books and was getting up from the table. There was that movement again, the one where she took a strand of hair and fixed it behind her ear. Just like yesterday morning, when he had first made the connection outside the restaurant. Charlie's heart ached. This was definitely not a feeling he was used to. What was it about this girl? More importantly, what had he done to upset her?

'Ah, Charlie, don't you like me anymore? You prefer to be with the Neapolitan pirate?' pouted Leonora, putting her face right up to his.

'Of course, I like you,' smiled Charlie; but as he tried to look around Leonora, she kept moving her head to block his view. Charlie grabbed her by the shoulders and moved her out of the way. At which point he noticed a scowling Nico storming out of the refectory. *Not again, Nico.* Charlie was getting a little bored with his tantrums; he didn't fancy Leonora and wouldn't do anything to hurt Nico's feelings, but the boy was always stropping off. Charlie's thoughts turned again to the girl with the sapphire-blue eyes, wearing the denim jacket and lace glove on her right hand. True, her fashion sense was a bit 1980s Madonna, but he could do retro. 'Why do you call her the Neapolitan Pirate?' he asked.

'I think Charlie's in love with the pirate,' teased Patricia, crooking her forefinger into a hook and waving it in Charlie's face. 'Have you never seen the film?'

'What, *Peter Pan*?'

Leonora punched Charlie in the arm. 'No, *The Neapolitan Pirate*! It's an Italian film. Never mind, if you knew the film you would understand why we say that Maria is the Pirate.'

Charlie rubbed his arm and gave Leonora wide mock-angry eyes. She stepped into him and took his hands. Charlie stared down at the hands he was holding. No lightning bolts. No fireworks or electric shocks. Just another girl, and it wouldn't matter if it was Rome or another planet, they were all the same to Charlie. Except the girl with sapphire-blue eyes.

'Do you love me, Charlie?'

Charlie shook his head. 'No, but Nico does.'

Leonora laughed. 'You're such a tease. Nico's a good friend, that's all…'

But Charlie wasn't listening. He was watching Maria's retreating figure. So cool: right hand in her pocket, the fingers of her left hand teasing loose strands of hair behind her ear.

Maria cast a quick glance back over her shoulder. *Wait*.

Charlie lifted his hand to stop her.

Too late – she had already turned her face and was walking out of the refectory.

VII

The trembling fingers beckon Maria. She follows down the narrow street, slipping on the grey cobbled stones, blinded by the rain. Mamma moves quickly. Silent steps. Maria tries her hardest to run, but her feet are like lead. Now, the rain is lashing down, stinging her face. Maria holds a hand up to shield her eyes. Focus. Where is she? Maria makes to run again, but the piazza is deserted. Where? Maria holds both hands up to her eyes. Only this time it is not the rain that causes her to blink blindly. White light. Two great orbs. A car horn wails. Maria screams and falls. The ground is hard and wet. Mamma holds out a shaking hand. Maria reaches out to grab it and then falls back down into a puddle.

Mamma is now stood at the top of the church steps. Maria scrambles to her feet and splashes across the piazza. She stands in front of the church, arms spread out wide. Where has she gone now? Mamma, please! Tears mingle with the raindrops streaming down her face. Maria turns. The car is heading straight for *her*, headlights hunting again out of the darkness. The car engine races as the driver hits the accelerator pedal. The car screeches a loud mournful wail. Maria opens her mouth to scream. Everything is a brilliant white.

The driver gets out of his car. He holds onto the door, not wanting to venture too close to the prostrate body. The driver looks up at the church steps. The Gattara stares. The driver gets back into the car. The car engine screams in protest as the mangled metal is reversed out of the piazza. Maria has seen all and nothing. She opens her eyes and screams.

Maria had woken up in a cold sweat. She had been having the same dream for the past week. It would soon be the anniversary of Mamma's death. The dream is so vivid, like it's trying to tell her something; but the driver's face is always in shadow. Maria looked at the picture of Mamma on her bedside cabinet. The black-and-white movie-star pose never fades; the beauty is great and eternal, like the pictures from her film's downstairs in the restaurant. It's as if Mamma was still alive, and not just her father in denial. But she isn't alive, she's been gone nearly a year: killed by a hit-and-run driver in the dead of the night.

Maria sat alone at a table in the refectory, trying to read one of her text books. Whilst the other students sat chatting and drinking coffee, she took the time to try and catch up with her studies. Despite the dwindling clientele, she found herself working longer hours to make up for Papa's lack of interest in the restaurant, and his life in general; and, her college work was suffering. Others would love to get her grades, but she knew she could do better, and she was beginning to resent having to work so hard to keep the family business ticking over while Papa was still lost in his grief. She chided herself for complaining about her poor father. Mamma's death had left him a broken man.

And there he was.

Maria looked up from her book and saw the boy with the floppy hair walking towards her table. She quickly looked back down and pretended to be consumed with her book. But Maria couldn't help herself from glancing back up – he was just so good looking. With his boy-band looks, it was like he had walked off the pages of a teen magazine. Maria realised they were both staring at each other.

Hello... Maria heard herself saying, her voice sounding high and distant. Her heart was racing. Calm down... her inner voice was chattering away at a hundred kilometres an hour. Maria gathered herself and carefully closed the book on her right hand.

'You're the girl from the restaurant in Via della Verita – yes?'

'You mean the pizzeria?' *Why had she not just said – 'Yes, I am'? It was a restaurant; why correct him. Even if it was technically a pizzeria, why did she have to correct him? Calm down Maria...*

'I take it that you work at the *pizzeria* to help pay for your education. I've seen you there a few times.' The boy had said a whole other bunch of stuff that she didn't understand.

'What are you? An English spy... or the Mr Sherlock Holmes, perhaps?' *What was she saying? Again, a simple 'yes' would have sufficed.*

'Let me see. Your name is... Wait, I know it – Maria!'

Maria's heart skipped a beat. How did he know her name? He wasn't in any of her classes, or and she wasn't a part of the ever-growing friendship group he seemed to be acquiring, which included Leonora and Patricia. Maria wanted to blurt out: *How do you know my name?* But she managed to put the brakes on her racing thoughts. 'You have quite a gift.'

'Elementary, my dear Maria.' That was funny; but instead of laughing, Maria pulled a face. *Pretend you have no idea what he is talking about.* It was time to try and play it cool.

'It's what Sherlock Holmes used to say to Watson... sorry, it was a bad joke.' Charlie sat down at the table.

'No, wait. I see...' *Elementare, mio caro Watson.* Maria laughed. 'No, I think it was a very good joke, Charlie.'

'Wait, how do you know *my* name?'

Maria felt herself blush. *Yes, Maria, how do you know his name? Could it be that you are taken by this English boy, a smitten kitten?* 'Everybody knows the *English*... I mean, you are Charlie from England... Your reputation goes before you.'

'All good, I hope.'

'No, I'm afraid it's not good. It is definitely all bad.' It was true he was getting a bit of a reputation amongst the girls, and the boys seemed to be growing a bit weary of this Englishman with his cool airs and casual manner. But Maria didn't care. She felt like an outsider, too.

Charlie sat back in his chair and opened his arms wide.

Maria laughed again – he had her giggling like a schoolgirl. 'Now it's my turn to make a joke.'

Charlie looked at Maria.

Maria lost herself in his sea-green eyes. Her mouth opened dumbly. *Like a fish!*

'How do you do, Maria.'

Charlie's action took Maria by surprise. She wasn't expecting him to do that. How very English. *But don't panic.* She put down her pencil and held out her left hand.

'Boy Scouts handshake?'

What?

'Left-handed. Apparently…'

What was he saying?

'The reason being that…' and then he was going on about a whole bunch of stuff, something to do with shields and warriors that she couldn't comprehend.

'Charlie, I have no idea what you're talking about?' Maria inwardly rebuked herself for using his name again. *Too familiar and too keen!*

Maria looked at the hand that Charlie was extending and shook it. It was excruciating. She felt so self-conscious, and then he wouldn't let go. Maria grew increasingly uncomfortable at Charlie's prolonged touch. It wasn't something she was used to, and a sense of panic gripped her.

'Charlie?'

'Yes?'

'Can I have my hand back, please?'

Charlie smiled. *He did have the most amazing eyes.* 'And I see that you play a musical instrument. The violin?'

It was like a thunderbolt had smashed down onto the table. *Why had he said that? Leonora – that's why. Trust her to go shooting her mouth off. God, how stupid she was to let her heart rule her head. Stupid, stupid kitten.* Maria wanted to scream.

'No, wait, the piano… perhaps?'

'Goodbye, Charlie.'

Maria didn't look up from her book. *Goodbye Charlie – just go!* Maria wanted to cry. *He was still standing there; why wouldn't he just go, and leave her alone?*

'Hello, Charlie! Where have you been?' *Leonora, right on cue.* 'Come on, Charlie,' said Leonora, taking hold of Charlie's arm and dragging him out of the chair without looking at Maria.

Maria packed up her books and got up from the table. She could feel her face burning red and wanted to get out of the refectory before anybody noticed. She brushed her hand across her face to wipe away any giveaway tears and swept a loose strand of hair behind her ear. *Just look at them*, she thought, as Leonora punched Charlie on the arm. Maria wished she was play-fighting with Charlie, but it would never be. Not now. Maria got up to go. Despite the hurt and anger she felt, she couldn't help but steal a quick glance back.

Charlie was looking at her over Leonora's shoulder with an imploring look.

Too late, thought Maria, and she turned her face and walked away.

Day 3

Nico's Scooter

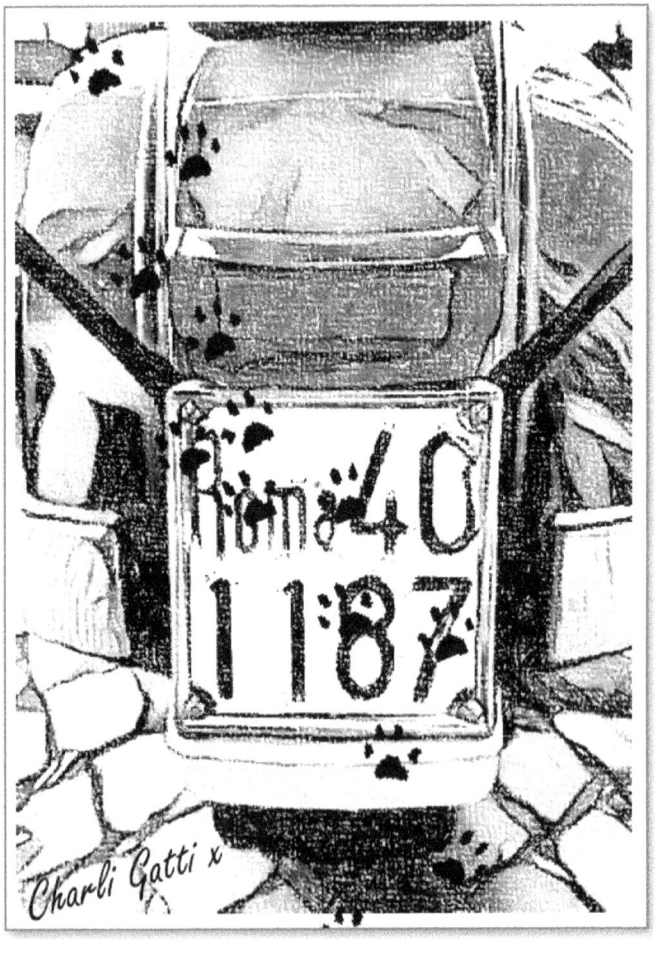

VIII

I'm back in the Spanish Quarter and running up a side street off Via Toledo. The flags are out, and Naples is waking up after the late afternoon siesta. Voices shout and hands reach out across the narrow streets. An empty wine bottle smashes on the cobbles and sends me spinning into a restaurant. A well-aimed pizza paddle swipes me back out onto the street and I'm running in the direction of the sea. Vesuvius rises up from the blue water, dark and familiar, and I look back to see the group of tomcats giving chase, and I'm darting in and out of the rush-hour traffic.

Beep!

Hey!

A Vespa scooter screeches to a stop, and the rider aims a kick at my tail. My lungs are bursting. The only sound I hear is the pulse-beat of my heart as it fills my head and ears. Now, I'm running blind through the shadows towards the small harbour near the Castle of the Egg, and then I leap into the darkening glare of sunlight…

Where'd she go?

You lost her!

No, you lost her! You were too slow.

What do you mean?

You had her back there in Mario's Pizzeria.

Look, down there.

Where?

By the fishing boats.

That's not her.

It is so.

No wonder you lost her, you don't even know who you're chasing after.

Come on, boys, let's go find her!

But that was then. I crouch down, tucking myself into a small hole in a wall. I listen. Thump-thump-thump. Just thinking about what happened puts me on edge and my heartbeat masks every other sound. Are they still out there, looking for me? I can't afford to sneak-a-peek out. I've over-stepped the mark this time. But Bruno wanted to kill *me*. What was I supposed to do? All this talk of *business*, it confuses me. What do I care about business? Only that it can get a street cat killed in Naples if you cross the line. And I have crossed the line. I don't know how, but somewhere I've stepped over the point of no return.

Now, I see the lights and the pretty girls. The boys whistle and the accordion player grins: his black and white teeth seem to stretch across his face and mirror the keys of his instrument. That voice. Such a beautiful voice. But such a harsh, brutal face. The music envelops the streets. Naples, in the evening sun, is alive.

A shadow.

Gigi Gatto looms over me.

He nods and I follow.

What's all this I hear about Bruno?

I shrug. News travels fast on these streets.

Good answer. I know that it's not true. At least, I hope it isn't, Bella.

I look past Gino. A dozen feline faces loom out of the shadows.

You know the one they call Pepe?

I nod.

Pepe is picking up some cargo at the dock's tomorrow afternoon; make sure you're on that lorry.

Okay.

And, Bella…

Yes?

Tomorrow you leave Naples… forever.

Either I leave, or I try to see things out here in Naples and probably die. But I didn't mean to hurt Bruno. It was his fault. He attacked *me*. I was tired and not thinking straight. I thought they were all going to kill me! I was tucked into the castle wall with my heart going boom-a-boom-boom, and there in the blackness was Bruno and his gang creeping up on me. They had chased me through the Spanish Quarter and down to the Castle of the Egg. I was hiding and they came up out of nowhere. Because that's their street-cat style. I tried to run out of the hole in the wall and towards the little fishing port and all the boats. And then I couldn't run anymore, because my way was blocked by fishing nets. I turned around. Two choices: either I fight a dozen wild cats, or I jump in the sea. There was no choice really – I had to fight. I braced myself and Bruno flew through the air.

Silence. A moment of perfect silence.

My heart stopped and Bruno was suspended in mid-flight. I had spun onto my back by the time he landed on top of me and I kicked. Hard, all four legs pumping as my feet connected with his hard-ribbed belly. The momentum took him, and he flew across the sky until I heard a great splosh! I got back up onto my feet and jumped onto the prow of a boat. Bruno was splashing at the water with his front paws, his head going under as he struggled to take great gulps of breath. The rest of the gang ran along the jetty, shouting, *Swim Bruno, swim!* Bruno kept hitting out at the water, but he was going further out to sea and disappearing under the water for longer periods.

Bruno!

I ran. I ran back through the fishing port, I ran past the people coming to see what the commotion was with all these mad cats jumping about on the jetty, and I ran up and away. I looked down from a high wall and saw the fisherman's hook scoop Bruno's body out of the water. A dozen angry cats turned, and in that moment, I knew I had broken the code.

I had killed another cat.

I can see that it was not your fault. The problem is Bruno's gang won't see it that way. You have to go away to Rome.

But why Rome?

I have a cousin up there; his name is Marco Del Vecchio. He'll look after you. He takes care of my business in the Eternal City.

Business.

Yes, Bella – business. And your business is now my business. You'll thank me for this. One day, somebody might come and ask you a favour in return, and that's how this business works. Now, come with us, you need to eat. You have a busy day tomorrow.

The next morning, I'm laid down in a box on top of a coarse blanket, surrounded by oranges. The smell reminds me of the Spanish Quarter, and I feel homesick. I sit up and look over the crates and see Vesuvius covered in black clouds, with Naples disappearing in the distance. And it starts to rain. The blue road sign points a big white arrow: *Roma*. I sleep a little. I wake a little. I gaze at unfamiliar landscapes: a monastery on the top of a mountain, castles in the sky. I sleep a little more…

When I wake the next time, I catch the eyes of the driver in the rear-view mirror.

Aargh!

Why is he screaming like that?

Good for nothing cat! Get out of my car!

Where am I? A mad face is screaming at me in the rear-view mirror. How did I get here? I must have been dreaming. I was back in Naples… The crazed man rips a plastic horn of life from the dashboard and it smacks into the leather upholstery just above my head.

What do you think you are doing in here? Get out!

The bloated face in the mirror is red with anger. Time to go, and I jump up and clamber through a little open window in the rear of the car. The man heaves his great bulk out of the driver's seat and begins to kick out at everything. My heart is beating wildly. It's still racing from the dream. Then the man starts to grab at tools from the workbench and throws something that clangs loud against the stone floor. Definitely not the time to be hanging about. There is a chink of yellow light at the far end of the garage and I run, but I'm blindly dodging manic kicks that seem to fizz past my ears. There is something clinging to my face and wrapping itself around my legs. I see a small chink of light and push through the gap in the door and tumble out into the street and safety.

The Gattara stops and I hide behind her skirts.

The Gattara pulls the silk off my face and untangles the fine material of the scarf that's wrapped itself around my legs.

The man stops in his tracks.

The Gattara walks off into the night, with me at her heel.

Day 4

Mini Cooper – *The Italian Job*

IX

Angelina Belletti. How best to describe her? The face of an angel, as her name suggests, but she doesn't come from any place like heaven that I know of. I'm walking across the Piazza della Rotonda, minding my own business, making my way to Toni's pizzeria.

'What brings you here, Spanish?' Angelina sits on her haunches and inspects a well-manicured paw.

Before I can answer, a dozen cats emerge from the shadows. They do not have faces of angels.

'Come, come… Has the cat got your tongue?' Angelina looks me directly in the eyes.

Now, I'm from Naples, which is a tough place to grow up, but these Roman cats are pretty tricky, and I haven't quite sussed them out yet. I'm figuring that Angelina considers me a threat to her relationship with Marco Del Vecchio. Why a beautiful pedigree Russian Blue would think that a tortoiseshell mismatch like me was any sort of competition for Marco's affections is anybody's guess; but she has an image to keep up, I suppose.

'Angelina, I'm just minding my own business, wandering about in the morning sun. I like the city in the early hours.' I am not going to say anything about the garage or being taken by the Gattara to the Torre Argentina Cat Sanctuary and being fed a handsome breakfast, because the street gangs consider that to be an *infamita*: an infamy of the worst kind; and I'm not going to mention getting chased out of the garage because, again, breaking and entering to find a warm place to sleep is also against the gang culture.

'Do you need a guide?' quips one of her gang.

'Or a map?' another says.

'Have you seen the Pope on his way to Mass?'

'Enough, girls!' Angelina speaks, and the faces retreat into the blackness. 'Don't mind them. It's just that you always wander about on your little lonesome – or with the other little crazies you call your friends – and I just don't know whether I can trust you, Bella.'

'Please, Angelina... I'm just a street cat from Naples trying to fit in here in Rome.'

'We're all street cats here. And we're all just trying to fit in somewhere,' Angelina smiles. There is a movement behind her and the faces creep out from the shadows again. 'Can I trust you, Spanish Bella?'

A slip of the tongue - an unguarded moment of intimacy, perhaps? The use of my name instead of just the mocking nickname: *Spanish*. But just as suddenly, Angelina is back to her usual cool self. Time to play along.

'You can trust me, Angelina.'

But before the words have left my mouth, she is gone.

X

Charlie looked out across the Piazza della Rotonda. It was earlier than usual. He had not slept well. The incident with Maria in the refectory kept playing over in his head. Why had she reacted so badly when he asked if she played an instrument? And why had Leonora and Patricia felt the need to be so awful and call her the Neapolitan Pirate? Charlie tousled his hair in an attempt to clear his brain. He watched as the cats emerged from the pillars and shadows of the Pantheon. Why were they all staring at the tortoiseshell cat? He was certain he had seen her in the Via della Verita. Was she the one that awful policeman had thrown a stone at? It couldn't be; there were thousands of street cats in Rome. But this cat was a tough little cookie. There was something about her that appeared to unnerve the others, they couldn't keep still and kept going back and forth, in and out of the shadows. Except the grey one. She looked for all the world as if she owned the Piazza.

And there she was... Maria!

Charlie went to call out, but before he could find his voice she'd disappeared into a butcher's shop. Charlie hurriedly scrambled into his clothes and dashed down the stairs. As he came crashing out of the entrance door to his apartment block, he had to break through a line of tourists.

Jeez!

No time for apologies. The Piazza was starting to come to life; the chaos and chatter were beginning to bubble.

Charlie ran across the piazza and then stopped dead in his tracks.

Maria came out of the butcher's shop holding a box in front of her. Charlie ducked behind a fruit stall and watched as she balanced the box against her chest. Now he knew why they had called her a pirate. How cruel were the words of Leonora and Patricia; why on earth did they think it was funny to joke about her… and it was no wonder Maria had got so cross at him. He really had no idea. Charlie had watched her working at the tables every morning for the past fortnight and had never noticed.

As Maria walked off Charlie broke cover and ran across to the butcher's shop.

'That girl…,' he said, as he burst through the door.

'Ah, the English student who owes me money… When you gonna pay?' asked the butcher, waving his meat cleaver at Charlie.

Charlie held up his hands. 'The sausage? Yes, I hadn't forgotten, really.'

'Really? Neither have I.'

'I'll pay you back this evening. Cash flow problem.'

'You gotta sell more pictures?'

Charlie nodded.

'When you paint the pictures that the tourists want to buy, then you sell the pictures. This is true.'

'Yes, sort of, I suppose – whatever. But the girl?'

'What girl?'

'The girl who was in here a minute ago - Maria.'

'What about her?'

'I go to college with her, and yesterday...'

'You like Maria, eh? Boys, this *English* he take the fancy to Maria; what do you think of that?'

Charlie found himself being stared at by two identical younger versions of the butcher, who stopped their chopping and preparations to look disdainfully over their shoulders at him.

'Let me tell you about Maria.' The butcher placed his cleaver down on the counter.

Charlie kept his eyes on the cleaver. He had heard that Italians can be very protective of their women but thought this was all just talk. Now, he wasn't quite so sure.

'Maria is the sweetest, most loving and hard-working girl in this district, you hear?'

Charlie nodded. 'I know. I watch her every day at the restaurant and I see her at college.'

The butcher held up his hands. The sons set down their knives. Charlie looked behind him at the open door, not sure if he should make a quick getaway.

'As I said, she is the sweetest girl in the district and a loving daughter to Toni. Her mother was so proud of her.'

Charlie caught the words. '*Was* so proud of her? Why is she not proud of her now?'

The butcher pointed upwards, and Charlie's gaze followed the bulbous finger and then settled on the butcher's face again. The butcher shook his head. 'It's tragic. One year ago, today. It's just not fair. That's all I'm saying.'

'Is that when Maria lost her hand?'

The butcher and his sons looked at each other and then back to Charlie.

'What are you talking about?' shouted the butcher, reaching for his cleaver.

'Maria's hand. I noticed when she walked out carrying the box, and that's why they called her the Neapolitan Pirate...'

'Who dared to call her this?'

'Two girls at college… it doesn't matter...'

CHOP!

The butcher brought his cleaver down hard on the counter, sending bits of meat and bone flying through the air. 'It's an outrage!'

Charlie started for the door.

'Wait!'

Charlie stopped.

'Tell me, *English*, do you think it is fair? The daughter of the most beautiful actress in Naples and a meek hard-working man like Toni is born without a hand? Is it God's way of saying there is too much beauty here? Did he think he would even things up a little? He giveth and then he taketh away. I was never a religious man...' – the butcher made the sign of the cross – 'but this made me think it is a cruel God that does this. But she is such a blessed child, so clever and so pretty.'

Charlie stared at the butcher. The sons turned back to their work. His head was spinning. He had to talk to Maria; he had to explain that he did not know that she only had one hand. He had only ever looked at her face, captivated by the light of her smile and the sapphire-blue of her eyes. Charlie felt sick.

'What's the matter, *English*, my sausage not good on the stomach?'

'No… I'm sorry. I'll bring your money this evening. *Grazie.*' Charlie made to walk out the door.

'Wait, English.'

Charlie turned to the butcher.

'Forget about the money. Pay me when you have made your millions. Now go; she'll be going to the flower shop in Largo del Teatro Valle. Today is a special day.' And the butcher made a sign of the cross again, which Charlie took as his cue to leave.

Charlie ran down the Via di Torre Argentina and took the Via de' Nari. He was running past the street artists with their easels and satchels as they headed towards the nearby Piazza Navona. Charlie raced through the narrow streets, dodging cars and scooters as he wended his way towards the Largo del Teatro Valle. At last, he came to a flower shop. The florist was outside, arranging her display.

'Maria? Has she been here yet?' Charlie blurted.

The flower seller gave him a quizzical look.

'Sorry...' In his haste, Charlie had reverted to speaking English. He repeated his question in Italian and was waved off in the general direction of the Piazza Navona. Charlie jogged, craning his neck to see if he could catch Maria amongst the foot traffic.

And there she was, heading towards the Via della Verita and *La Margherita.* Charlie stopped and watched Maria greet the old man with the moustaches, offering her cheeks up for the obligatory kisses. They talked. The old man wiped a tear from his face and Maria shook her head. Then she nodded to the table next to the door and disappeared inside the restaurant. Charlie dashed across the road. When he reached the door to the restaurant, he put his hands through the multi-coloured plastic bug blinds and went to walk in.

'Wait,' said the old man; 'the restaurant is closed this morning.'

'Closed?'

'*Si*, closed.'

'But you're here, in your usual seat. Same as ever.'

The old man put his newspaper down on the table and wiped his face with his bare hand. 'That's true, but it's still closed.' The old man waved him inside.

Charlie walked in through the bug blinds. He looked about the empty restaurant, at the perfectly laid tables and the clay pizza oven. The coffee machine sat silent. Charlie gazed at the black and white photos and film posters that adorned the walls. The features were the same, and there was no mistaking the likeness. The butcher was right: Maria's mother was beautiful, and she was the spitting grown-up image of her daughter. The photographs, newspaper clippings and memorabilia gave a snapshot history of the life of a screen idol: '*Bella Valeria Viola*', '*Ciao Vivi*', '*La Dea – the goddess.*'

'What are you doing in here?'

Charlie started. 'Maria, forgive me. I came here to apologise.'

'Apologise about what?' Maria walked behind the counter and the coffee machine hissed into life.

'About yesterday in the refectory.'

'It's nothing; please forget it.'

'No, I didn't realise. I suppose, as an artist, I should be more observant, but... these pictures are amazing. Your mother?'

Maria nodded and busied herself with Amerigo's cappuccino.

'She is very beautiful.'

'My mother's dead, Charlie.' Maria stared hard at Charlie, her blue eyes turning a colder shade of grey.

'I'm sorry. I didn't know until the butcher told me...'

Maria came out from behind the counter and carried the steaming cup outside to Amerigo. Charlie followed her.

'Wait, Maria! What day is it?'

'Wednesday,' answered Amerigo.

'No, what date...?' Charlie grabbed at Amerigo's newspaper and read the date. 'The 13th of August. I'd completely forgotten!' Maria and Amerigo both frowned at Charlie. 'It's exactly one year ago today that my father died.'

Maria's mouth dropped.

Amerigo wiped again at his moustaches as the tears streamed down his face.

'Another one of your jokes, Charlie?'

'I'm sorry?'

'Stop saying you're *sorry*. You are quite possibly the most horrible person I have ever met. How dare you come here with your sick jokes on today of all days?' Maria flung her apron on the ground and ran inside, barging past Charlie. Amerigo muttered under his breath and looked to the heavens.

Charlie went back inside and found Maria standing at the far end of the restaurant, with her back to him. The movement of her shoulders told him that she was crying. Charlie walked towards her.

Maria spun round quickly, her eyes wild and wet. 'Why do you say these things? I thought you were somebody I could get to know and like. Heaven knows why. I'm just a stupid… smitten-kitten, I suppose. Now I know that you are just like the others. You're as mean as all of them, Charlie – only worse!'

Charlie held Maria's apron out to her. She snatched it from him, sat down at a table and buried her face in the white cloth.

'Maria, please tell me what happened to your mother.'

Maria shook her head.

Charlie sat down opposite Maria. 'Okay, my story... My father died in a car accident. He was with his mistress. They were driving back from a weekend in London when a lorry ploughed into the back of them. They both died instantly. That's the reason I'm here. I spent the whole of Upper-Sixth at College fighting the world; I realised that I had to get away to sort my head out and find what I really wanted to do. My love of art and Italy brought me to Rome, and that's how I ended up at the *Accademia*, and all roads appear to have led me to you... Which sounds a bit rubbish really. And now, without meaning to, I have hurt and upset you. I didn't mean to, really... That's not me. That's not what I'm about. Truly.'

Maria lifted her head. She looked abstractedly at the walls and shook her head. 'It was one year ago today that my mother was murdered.' Charlie's face must have betrayed the shock of what she had just said. 'Really, just like your father. It was the 13th of August. Romano had come around in the evening and bawled at Papa. He was calling him all the names under the sun, threatening to close the business and leave him penniless and without a wife. My father is not a weak man, but Romano is a bully. He used to work in our kitchen as a teenager – that's him in that clipping there...'

There was no mistaking the broad face and awkward features; the newspaper article spoke of how the teenaged kitchen-hand had, with the help of the great Neapolitan actress, overcome his shyness and secured a position with the Rome City Police.

'That was nearly eighteen years ago. My mother was pregnant with me – although she didn't know it at the time. Romano did his national service in the army and then spent the first fifteen years of his police service working the other districts of the city. Then, just over a year ago, he came back. The shy, awkward boy had grown into this loud monster of a bully. Get this, he came back and tried to woo his boyhood crush – my mother – and made my father's life a misery. Now, I forget... where was I?'

'You were saying that Romano had been threatening to close the business...'

'Yes, thank you. So, my father kicks him out of the restaurant. As I said, my father is not a weak man. He is a proud Neapolitan – it is only now that he seems like a broken shell... My mother said she was going to have it out with Romano. My father tells her no. But my mother was as stubborn as she was beautiful. It was a filthy night and the rain was pouring down. I remember her tying the silk scarf around her head. It was the navy blue and yellow scarf with black cats in the pattern; my father had bought it for her in London when they went there at the height of her fame. I loved to wear that scarf and pretend I was Mamma in the films.' Maria laughed at the memory. 'So, then she took the bicycle and made her way over to Romano's flat. Later that night, the police called. There had been an accident and my mother had been found knocked down in the road. The driver didn't stop. They still don't know who killed her. And they never found the scarf.' Maria nodded at a large black and white picture. Valeria Viola was dressed in a dark-coloured shift dress and wore a silk scarf with little cats in the pattern around her neck. 'This morning we are going over to the cemetery.'

'Maria, I'm so sorry...'

'No, I'm sorry; you weren't to know. But your father, too?'

'My father and mother didn't love each other the way your parents did. There was no time for love in my childhood. Too busy in England for such things, I'm afraid...'

From the look on Maria's face, it was clear that she didn't understand. How could families not love each other? That was what life was all about, surely?

Just then, there was a commotion with Amerigo. Maria and Charlie made their way outside.

'We are closed!'

'But we would like coffee from the famous *La Margherita Pizzeria*. We are big fans of Valeria Viola. It's on our schedule. You have cappuccino froth all over your whiskers, so it must be open.' A sweaty-faced man holding a long, thin carbon stick with a red baseball pennant was with a group of expectant tourists, some of whom were taking their seats at the pavement tables.

'Due to unforeseen circumstances, we are closed...'

'No, wait!' Charlie shouted. He turned to Maria. 'How much will you pay me to keep the place open, serving coffee, while you are at the cemetery? I mean, I'm not going to sell any pictures this morning...'

'You never sell any pictures,' muttered Amerigo.

'Amerigo, where are your manners?' Maria laughed. 'Please sit down, everybody; we'll take your orders shortly.'

Charlie said, 'What are you laughing at? A joke, perhaps, Maria?'

Maria turned.

A smiling face.

'No, Charlie. But is this offer to serve, another of *your* jokes?'

'No. I used to have a Saturday job in a coffee shop back home. I am a trained barista.'

'Really? That's all very well and good, but can you make *real* Italian coffee?'

Charlie went behind the counter and set to work at the *Gaggia* machine. He loaded the portafilter with coffee and tamped down on the counter to compact the brown powder granules. He loaded the portafilter into the machine, placed a cup underneath the spout and pressed the button. Whilst he waited for the brown liquid to drip down, he filled a metal jug with some milk and held this up to the frothing wand. Charlie flicked a switch and smiled as the machine spluttered and steamed into life. He hadn't lost it. Charlie stole a glance over his shoulder, and Maria nodded appreciatively. Setting the cup down on a saucer, Charlie spooned the bubbling milk into the cup; he finished off with a quick swoosh of the jug and the froth swirled around the top of the cup as he glided it across the counter. Maria regarded the offering with a critical eye.

'*Perfetto*! Now all we need are another dozen *cappuccini* and a double *espresso* for the tour guide. Come on, get to work, chop-chop!' Maria whizzed on her apron and was out of the door, taking orders.

Charlie smiled. Today was not going to be just another day in Rome.

XI

Charlie sat at the table, reading Amerigo's newspaper. It was funny how hard it was sometimes to grasp the true translation of the words on the page. Truth be told, his A-Level Italian enabled him to more than get by, and he understood most of what people said to him; but there were many words that he guessed at; and, once people realised, he was English, the conversation tended to swing from one language to the other, depending on the message that needed to be conveyed.

'I expect you're feeling pretty good about yourself?' the old man said, as he puffed at his cigarette.

'It's the first money I've properly earned since I've been here.'

'Really? Do you know why this place is called *La Margherita*?' The old man didn't wait for Charlie to answer. 'I'll tell you. Toni and Valeria come from Naples, which is the home of pizza. Now, in 1889, some years after the unification of Italy, King Umberto the First and Queen Margherita visited Naples. They say that a local chef created a pizza representing the colours of the Italian flag: red tomato sauce, white buffalo mozzarella cheese, and green basil leaves. This little pizzeria is named after the famous Neapolitan pizza. I bet you didn't know that, young man.'

'I didn't. Thank you for the history lesson.'

The old man ignored the sarcasm in Charlie's voice. 'This pizzeria has been here over twenty years. They opened it after Valeria was sacked by her film studio. She came to Rome to be a star and ended up working in a restaurant. And you know why that happened?' The old man jabbed at the air with his cigarette. 'Because she refused to give up her husband.'

'I don't understand.'

'The studio wanted to keep Toni quiet. Here was this glamorous actress from Naples, about to take Rome and the *Cinecittà* Studios by storm – and they dropped her just like that!' Amerigo snapped his fingers. 'They wanted her to be photographed with all her romantic leads and keep her husband in a closet. Then the Neapolitan temper kicked in, and that was the end of her film career. Valeria was so loyal to Toni. You know, they sacked her whilst they were on a weekend break in London. Toni had bought her this scarf with cats on it. The cats reminded her of Naples, or something like that anyway – I've never been one for cats myself – and she wore that on the day she was sacked from the studio and every day thereafter without fail. It was as if it was a reminder to Valeria of both love and treachery.'

Charlie pondered on the story and thought how different the relationship of Maria's parents had been to that of his own. It was just like something in the movies.

'She'll never fall in love with you.'

Charlie was quickly brought out of his reverie. 'Who?'

'Maria, you young fool. You know that, don't you? She's wedded to this place. Like her mother before her, she'll look after Toni to the last. That will be a long time: these Neapolitans live forever. Besides, she's in love with me.' The old man cackled and then coughed over his shoulder.

This old man was a strange fish. He was a constant presence, with his yellow whiskers and newspaper. Charlie couldn't recall having not seen him sat outside *La Margherita*. He was a cantankerous old whatnot, that much was certain.

'But I'll tell you a secret,' and Amerigo leaned forward so that the customers sat at a nearby table couldn't overhear. 'Don't talk to her about her disability. She may hide it well, but that's because she doesn't like to draw attention to herself. She's a modest beauty, like her mother. You apologised earlier. Now let it go. She'll like you the better for it. Did you really not love your father?'

The question caught Charlie off guard. This old man was no fool; he took in everything. 'My father didn't love me. Neither does my mother, really. To her, I simply exist.' Charlie turned his attention to the newspaper.

'That is very sad to hear. Is that an English thing, to not love one's own family?'

Charlie considered the question. 'No, it's not an English thing. It's just a my-family thing. It's no big deal, really.'

'Really? It's a big enough deal to bring you to Rome. What exactly are you running from?' When Charlie didn't reply, Amerigo continued, 'Do you want to know about Maria's disability?' Amerigo pulled the newspaper down and looked Charlie in the eye. 'Some say it is an act of God, but Valeria told me that it runs in the female side of her family. It seems to have skipped a generation with Valeria. They call it *Amelia*, and it's a birth defect where the baby is born without a limb; or, as in Maria's case, her right hand. It didn't seem to bother her as a young child, but as she has got older, she has become more conscious of it. She is a very beautiful young woman, hard-working and loyal to her father. But I sense a melancholy about her now. I won't allow anyone to hurt her.' Amerigo pointed a finger at Charlie.

Charlie blew out his cheeks. How much had his words hurt her yesterday? *Bad joke, Charlie.* And the cruel words of Leonora and Patricia – had she heard them too?

'She used to be best friends with those two. But since they became teenagers, and got interested in boys and parties, they ignore her and mock her.'

What was it with the old man? Was he a mind reader, too?

'Charlie!'

Leonora.

'Charlie boy!'

Patricia.

The old man got up and walked off to collect dirty cups.

Charlie turned. Not a mind reader at all, just a very observant old man.

Leonora sat down at the table and pouted. 'Are you coming to the party tonight, Charlie? You can come with me.'

Patricia clapped Charlie on the shoulders. 'He's going with me, silly. You're going with Nico.'

Leonora mimed sticking her fingers down her throat.

Charlie got up. Was there no limit to this girl? How could she be so rude about Nico? He worshipped her – and that's the problem. If Nico didn't dote on Leonora so much, she would respect him all the more for it.

'Where are you going, Charlie?'

'To work.'

Leonora and Patricia stared at each other.

Patricia said, 'You work here?'

Charlie nodded. 'Sure do.'

Leonora rose and stood with hands on hips. She chewed violently at the piece of gum in her mouth. 'So, what about the party?'

Charlie shrugged.

'Suit yourself. Come on, Patricia; let's leave the *English* to his Neapolitan Pirate.' Leonora turned her nose to the air and made to leave. As she did so, Amerigo tripped over a chair and the dregs of the coffee cups he was holding flew through the air and were deposited on the two girls' clothing.

'Clumsy old man!' Patricia shouted.

Leonora shouted something that Charlie recognised as an expletive in the Roman dialect.

'Oops...' Amerigo winked at Charlie.

The two girls stropped off across the piazza like wounded prima donnas.

'What have we here, eh? What have we here?' boomed Romano. 'The artist as a young man becomes the dish washer. Ah, you have found your true talent at last.'

'It seems we have something in common,' quipped Charlie.

'Oops...' Amerigo ducked down and sat in his chair.

Romano looked Charlie up and down. 'You think you're clever, eh? Think that Romano is a little slow up here.' He tapped the side of his head. 'I'm watching you, *English*. Mark my words. What are you doing here anyway? Where's Toni and Maria?'

'You forget what day it is?' Amerigo tapped the side of his head.

'Stupid old man, of course I haven't forgotten...' A vacant and lost look came over Romano's heavy features. He took off his hat and went into the pizzeria. Charlie stood in the doorway and pulled the bug blinds apart. Romano walked around the dining area, looking at all the pictures and clippings. He eventually came to the article featuring himself and took the black wooden photo frame from the wall. Unaware he was being watched, Romano whispered, 'My love. If it was not for that weak fool of a husband, you'd still be alive today.' Romano kissed the glass.

Charlie coughed.

Romano muttered under his breath. He carefully placed the frame back on the wall, took out his handkerchief and wiped the glass. Then he stepped back and pushed at one edge to satisfy himself that the frame was level. Romano walked towards the door. Charlie stepped back out of the way and Romano emerged onto the pavement. The policeman placed his hat on his head and walked off in the direction of Piazza Navona.

Charlie turned to Amerigo. 'What was that about?'

Amerigo tapped the side of his head. '*Pazzo* – he's completely and utterly mad. He's been infatuated with Valeria Viola since he was a boy. Since her death, he has treated Toni like dirt. If I was twenty years younger, I'd give him a good hiding.'

'Give who a good hiding?' Maria asked. 'Papa, why don't you go inside and have a lie down? I can take care of everything.'

Having returned from the cemetery Toni looked even older than Amerigo. The pain was written all over his ashen face, and the hunched shoulders betrayed his endless grief. Poor man thought Charlie. He watched Maria helping her father over the threshold and felt his own heartache. A sudden great sense of loss descended on him and made his head feel light.

'Are you okay, Charlie?'

Charlie looked at his phone and checked the date and time. 'Yeah, I'm fine...'

Maria reached out and touched his arm. 'Are you sure you're okay? You look very pale.'

'Nothing, really. I just remembered that I've got some work to hand in at the *Accademia*. I need to get the money for my exhibition piece and stuff, and... I'll see you later, at the party, perhaps... maybe.'

Maria watched Charlie cross the street.

Amerigo tapped the side of his head.

Charlie broke into a run as the tears he had denied for nearly a year finally came.

XII

Romano's grief fuelled his anger. No wonder he couldn't sleep last night. It was as if he had tried to erase the date from his memory. One year to the day since his great love had perished, and it was all the fault of that pathetic weak husband of hers. Why couldn't she have seen that? It was obvious, to Romano, that she needed a real man in her life. So, what if she was much older than him? He had loved her since he was a boy. He would love her forever, and he would take his revenge on Toni.

Romano was quickly brought back to the real world. Two hoodlums were throwing stones at cats, and the screams of a group of schoolchildren pierced through his melancholy.

What now?

Romano ran and took a hold of the thugs and dragged them into a doorway.

Romano breathed heavily. 'What on earth do you think you are doing?'

'But, uncle, you told us to chase the cats away,' spluttered the smaller of the youths. He was called Tito. He was seventeen years old, with a pointed face and a scar on his top lip. He had been roaming the streets of Rome all his life.

'Yes, uncle. You said: *If you love your Mamma, then chase the cats*,' panted the second boy. His name was Fino; he was a year older than his brother, and he had thick, black, curly hair. His AS Roma football top was tattered, and his jeans were torn at the knees.

Romano looked over his shoulder. 'The show's over, folks. I'll deal with these two urchins.'

The group of children was led away by their teacher, casting anxious glances at the cats who sought shelter down a side street.

Romano took hold of both boys by the ear and pushed their heads together.

'Ow!'

'Uncle, you're hurting.'

'I swear that if you weren't my own sister Paola's boys, I'd have thrown you in the Tiber by now and drowned you both, like a pair of worthless cats! What did I tell you?'

'To chase the cats, uncle...'

'Yeah, you told us to chase the cats…'

'I told you to *chase* the cats out of the Piazza Paradiso and into the Via della Verita. I didn't ask you to *stone* them. I didn't say *kill* them. I said *chase* them away from your mamma's restaurant when people weren't looking!'

The boys looked at each other with dumb expressions.

Romano pushed their heads together harder. 'Listen to me carefully, one last time. It's simple. The Via della Verita gets overrun with cats and I get to close down all the restaurants, including Toni's little pizzeria. At the same time, your mamma's restaurant thrives, and I… I mean, *we* all get rich. Do you understand?'

'Yes, uncle.'

'*Si*, uncle.'

'So, no more public stoning, okay? We do not *kill* the cats. We need them, got it? Besides, if your mother finds out that you've been hurting them, we'll all be for the high jump.'

The boys nodded. Romano sent them on their way with a slap round their heads. The passing crowd nodded at this display of zero-tolerance-no-nonsense policing. Romano had got his men and meted out swift retribution. Bravo.

Romano walked back along the Via della Verita, forgetting that he was originally heading towards the Piazza Navona. *Those oafs! One day they will bring much trouble to my doorstep and ruin everything.* For Romano had a master plan, a deceptively simple and yet wonderfully effective master plan – at least, he thought as much. And this plan would make him rich. All he had to do was keep flooding the local streets with cats, and the little known, or used, by-law about the restaurant owners not feeding feral cats would permit him to close their businesses indefinitely. But he had to catch them at it first. This catching them in the act had proved a little problematic with some, including Toni. The Neapolitan was wily. With others it had been easy. A bowl of scraps left outside late at night was enough for the closure notice to be slapped on the door. But Toni Viola always had an excuse: *They take it out of the bins in Via Governo Vecchio, Romano, and bring it here...* That was the best one. And he had locks on his rubbish bins. That was clever. But Toni would lapse, and it would only take one little window of opportunity and bang! A closure notice fixed to the door of *La Margherita*, and Romano would have exacted his revenge.

The Comandante had been sceptical at first: 'What about the rats?' he had asked.

'No, Comandante, it is the *cats* we are after, they are the real vermin.

'But won't the absence of cats attract the rats to the area?'

'Oh, no, Comandante, the clean-up will render the district the envy of the Eternal City.'

The Comandante had shaken his head; he didn't appear convinced. But Romano would show him and gain promotion to the next rank. Of course, there was a far bigger ulterior motive. There always was with Romano. The truth, he owned seventy-five percent of his sister's restaurant. *La Rosa Nera* – The Black Rose – was named after Valeria Viola's most famous film, and it was the first time she had played the part of the Neapolitan female pirate. Paola's restaurant was located a few hundred metres from Toni's pizzeria in the Piazza del Paradiso, it was amazing that nobody had realised that Romano was involved in the business. But there were other bars and restaurants named after the movies of Valeria Viola in the city: *The Gypsy*; *Roman Palace*; *The Flower of Naples*; and, of course – *The Neapolitan Pirate*. Besides, Romano's was a humble establishment. I mean, how much could he afford on a policeman's wages? But once all the competition had been closed down, it would give him a window of opportunity – that delicious, sweet phrase again – to build a client base. Ever since his days working as a kitchen-hand at *La Margherita*, Romano had dreamt of his own restaurant. All he had to do now was wait…

But wait… what was that?

Romano skulked into the shadows, trying desperately to blend into the background.

There…

Romano took his mobile phone from his pocket and swiped the screen to bring up the camera function. He zoomed in. *There* – as clear as day – was the old fool, Amerigo, feeding that damned tortoiseshell cat scraps from his own plate. Now, the by-law did not extend to the customers feeding the cats, even though Romano would tell them otherwise. This was just another way of reinforcing *his* by-law, a little reminder to all the restaurant and bar owners. A little warning, a parting shot across the bows, as it were. But hadn't he seen Amerigo working the tables with that English student this morning? Yes, technically that makes him unpaid help – a worker!

Romano felt inside the breast pocket of his tunic, and then looked up and down the Via della Verita. The blackened and boarded windows stared back at him. Romano tugged at the single sheet of paper, removed it from his pocket, and opened it up carefully - as if he were handling a treasured document from the Vatican museums. But the simple message written in bold black ink was more important to Romano than any of the Papal papers:

You are hereby informed that this restaurant is closed forthwith until further notice. By order of the Comandante of Police and issued by the Rome City Police.

Romano peeled the backing paper from the closure notice and marched across the Via della Verita.

XIII

The rain stopped. The coffin glistened wet in the shallow grave. A son reunited with his not-so-beloved parents. Charlie looked up at the mourners. Black is the new black. Designer sunglasses were fetched from handbags, coat pockets, or removed from the top of the head with a shake of well-groomed hair as sunlight flooded the cemetery. Not a dry eye in the house. What a show these people put on for themselves. The air-kisses and consoling pats on the arm were a well-rehearsed approximation of grief. There it was again, the restless apathy that Charlie felt towards everything that his parents, and all their friends, had ever contrived to be; that empty feeling bubbled once more to the surface as his father's funeral reached its climax.

And there she was. Charlie watched as his mother dabbed at the space between the *Ray Bans* and her right eye. He saw her reach behind and shake the thrusting hands that were offering fresh tissues as the graveside gatherers vied for grieving rights. She did this without turning. This woman was not for mourning. Charlie looked at his mother closely. There were no tears. Just a fortuitous raindrop from a sympathetic umbrella held aloft over the tragic widow. Charlie swallowed. He struggled to contain his simmering anger. Then he looked at Bess, and in her solemn face he saw his feelings mirrored. Two school years his junior, but a thousand times wiser than he. They both knew. They knew that everything about today was just like every other lie their parents had told. But Bess wouldn't allow the dutiful mask she wore to betray her inner feelings.

Cynthia placed a gloved hand on Charlie's arm. Her scent blended perfectly with the perfume of the flowers and bouquets propped up against the gravestones; and then she pressed herself against Charlie and air-kissed his cheeks. *Poor, sweet, darling boy. If you ever… ever need to talk. I know what it's like to lose your father, especially at such a young age. Take care, darling. Call me. Ciao!* Charlie liked Cynthia's affectations. True, she was awful, but she didn't take herself too seriously and was very funny with it. A squeeze of his arm and she was off, mingling with the crowd. The other mourners stood obediently in line as the ritual drew to an end. His mother stood with closed fists, clutching bunches of tissues. People smiled sympathetic nods at Charlie and Bess; bland condolences and empty words:

Call me if you ever need to talk. Cynthia again. Talk about what?

Talk about the fact that his father had died in a car crash with his lover. Talk about his mother standing at the graveside next to Roger, her beau. Talk about the dead son who had to be buried with the parents he despised – the family plot and all that. Talk about how privilege brings you nothing but lies and emptiness. Let's talk about *that*, shall we? There would be no tears before bedtime for Charlie. No outward signs of any emotion. This was not a display of bravado. Charlie stood at his father's graveside and realised that he simply felt *nothing*. He looked at his mother. For her, he felt nothing but contempt, mixed with a dash of loathing. A real monster of a woman, who had lived a thousand lies every day of her pampered life. Why *should* he care? Charlie looked at Bess. How easily she accepted the platitudes and the sympathetic kisses. One day she would be the Prime Minister or something equally as self-important, because Bess could ignore the lies and carry on with her life, regardless.

Charlie had carried on his own life in blissful ignorance, until Cynthia had dropped the bomb. Cynthia, his mother's oldest friend, who spent her whole life pretending to be the very person she actually was a helicopter-mum, gym-bunny, coffee-in-town-darling, dinner-at-ours, etc. *Darling…* You didn't have to look hard to see through all the pretence. It was hung like a sign around her neck: *Keep Calm and DO Carry On – Now, there's a Darling!* But Cynthia was funny in her own inimitable way. His mother wasn't like that at all. She just kept on trying to deceive everybody with the façade of playing the doting wife and mother. *Careless talk costs lives.* And bone-idle chatter can change lives forever. And when Cynthia did the chattering, his mother's make-believe world came crashing down. Come to think of it, Charlie had a lot to thank Cynthia for. She had played a deft hand.

Then, the sympathetic hands were thrust in his direction. Charlie hated the spotlight; unlike Bess, he never wanted to be near centre-stage. But there it was: *Sorry about the old man… If there's anything I can do… I remember when my grandfather died… You mustn't listen to what people say… He was a good man…* Enough. The circumstances surrounding his father's death had been the talk of the school, the talk of the town; it made the front page of the local paper. It had even featured in the *Daily Mail.* Yes, it was out there in all its glory: 'Car crash victims were LOVERS'.

The day after it happened, their mother had sat on the sofa while Charlie and Bess stood looking down at her. It all came out in one long blubbing confession.

But, despite everything, we've always been good parents, to both of you – haven't we?

Roger stood next to her, a comforting hand massaging her shoulder. The king is dead. Long live Roger. Charlie felt a menacing presence. His father's death was something he could deal with. But the threat posed by his successor so soon after the event could not be underestimated. His mother wouldn't see that. All she saw was a safe pair of hands to guide her future. She wouldn't be able to make it alone. She needed her social circle, needed to fit in, and needed a man in her life to give it any sense of purpose or direction. Charlie and Bess could give her nothing now. It was as if they, too, were dead to her.

Don't you have your own family to go home to?
Now look here, young man…

No, Roger, he's upset – about his father. He doesn't mean anything by it.

But Charlie did mean it, and he hadn't spoken to Roger since that day. Now Roger stood next to his mother at the graveside as she tried her very best to play her dutiful part; he was *the* strong arm to lean on, and he had a controlling hand on the till. Crocodile tears for her new hunter-gatherer. He wondered if his mother knew she was just a cash cow.

Charlie wandered into the crowd.

Cynthia?

Yes, darling.

Your ex-husband's a lawyer, isn't he?

Yes, darling, a complete… well, let's just say he is a very horrid man.

I may need some advice.

Then you've come to the right person.

I need to talk to somebody about inheritance.

The tears that filled his eyes at Amerigo's words had come thick and fast. It wasn't until he had reached his apartment that Charlie had been able to properly compose himself. He plugged his phone into the charger and sent a message to his mother: *Thinking of you, Charlie x.* Whatever, he needed the money. He could just imagine Roger's reaction; after all, it was Roger who had ensured that all of his father's estate had gone to Charlie's mother, effectively writing him and Bess out of the will. He already spent all the money they'd given to him for his stay in Rome, mostly on parties and a little on food and art materials. Now he needed two hundred euros to enter the end-of-course exhibition that was to be held at the Colosseum. The showcase would attract the top gallery owners and maybe his talent would be discovered. More importantly, the winner got a fully funded year of study at the *Accademia*. Charlie wasn't ready to go home just yet. He lay on his bed and waited for the phone to charge and his mother's reply.

It never came.

An hour later and Charlie was walking down the Via dei Fori Imperiali and heading towards the Roman Forum. His mother had not responded, and he just had to get some inspiration for his pictures in order to earn some money. As a student, Charlie had free access to all the major attractions, and he set about his work with great industry. There was no time to lose; he had to get some new pictures completed in order to earn his exhibition fee. It was a hot day. Charlie worked hard, his pencil moving as if with a mind of its own across the page. Once he had completed half a dozen A4-sized sketches and added a little watercolour paint to offset the monochrome, he headed back to the Via dei Fori Imperiali and took his place near to the other artists. If you can't beat them, join them. Charlie had over a dozen sketches, and he decided that if he reduced the price of each sketch to ten euros, he would be able to pay half the entrance fee tomorrow morning and then get back out on the street to earn the rest. He was leaving things late, but if he worked at some new sketches whilst he sat selling the others, then he might even have the money to get to Leonora's party this evening.

Things went well. By two o'clock, Charlie had sold four sketches and completed another two drawings. The other artists looked on with admiration at this young student, who seemed to be on a bit of a mission. Except one - there was always one. The one who you never saw drawing or painting a new picture because he was selling computerised images, and just dabbed or pretended to colour an unfinished piece.

'You trying to put me to shame?' whispered the man.

'Why should I do that?' answered Charlie, politely.

'Oh, I don't know. Maybe you think you are clever and want to take my business. This is my spot, after all.' The man had bad teeth and spoke with an accent. He wasn't Italian. This marked him out as particularly desperate and dangerous.

'I'll tell you what, I'll move along a bit. Then you can have your spot all to yourself.' Charlie didn't need the aggravation.

'I like your attitude.'

Charlie smiled. *Whatever*, he said under his breath.

Charlie walked along the road towards the Colosseum. It was ironic that he was trying to earn the money to pay his entrance fee in the shadow of Rome's most iconic monument, the very place that the exhibition would take place.

'I say... wait!'

Charlie heard the voice but carried on walking.

'Young man...' The voice carried over the rumble of the traffic and tooting of car horns.

Charlie carried on. He didn't want any trouble. Not today.

'Excuse me...'

Charlie felt the hand grab at his shoulder. He shrugged away.

'Wait!' shouted an American voice.

Charlie turned and saw a man take his *Let's Go Mets* baseball cap off his head and wipe his sweating brow with his forearm. 'I'm sorry, I didn't mean to startle you,' said the man, catching his breath. He waved his arm into the crowd. 'My wife asked me to catch up with you. Apparently, you are a talented new artist.'

Charlie looked into the swarm of tourists and recognised the woman with the floppy hat. She clutched at the hand of her son, who today was wearing a blue t-shirt with the word *Roma* written in the green, white and red of the Italian flag.

'I said to my husband that I had seen you near the Piazza Navona yesterday and how marvellous your pictures were. We were watching you sketch back there, and it is so refreshing to see art being created. It's quite obvious that most of the other images are fakes.' The woman smiled at Charlie. 'Please, can I show my husband?'

'Of course, here…' Charlie handed his portfolio over to the man and his wife pointed at the pictures.

Charlie looked at the boy. 'How do you like Rome?'

The boy hid behind his mother's skirts.

'I'm afraid he doesn't have speech. He's autistic.'

Charlie smiled at the boy and handed him a sketch pad and pencil. The boy drew a picture of a cat and handed the pad back. Charlie quickly sketched the Colosseum in the background and offered the pad again. The boy drew another cat.

'You like cats?'

'He loves cats,' said the woman.

Charlie tore the page from the sketchpad and handed the picture to the boy.

'We'll take them all,' said the man. 'How much?'

'I'm sorry, what?'

'We'll take them. Are they all signed?' The man shuffled through the sketches. 'They seem to be… and dated, too.'

The boy held his picture out to Charlie.

'I don't think you've signed this one,' laughed the woman.

Charlie scribbled his signature on the page.

'Will you take two hundred?' asked the man.

'Two hundred euros?' Charlie didn't mean to shout.

'Yes. I mean, there are, what, like fifteen sketches here…'

'Sixteen,' corrected the woman, pointing to the sketch that the boy was closely examining.

'Sixteen.' said the man, tousling the boy's hair. 'I mean, that's ten euros for each piece and a little for your time and effort. They really are very good.'

'Wow! That would be *amazing* – it's a deal!' Charlie could barely contain his excitement.

The man held out his hand.

Charlie shook it. 'Thank you.'

'Excellent. My wife has all the money. What was the name?' said the man, scrutinising Charlie's signature.

'Charlie Weller.'

'Ah, yes, Charles Weller. Take a tip, son. Sign yourself *Charles* in future. It'll make you sound more like a serious artist. There's a heck of a lot of small-time *Charlies* out there.'

Charlie gave his best smile. 'Charles it is, then.'

'Here, take this. Thank you so much.' The woman waved the banknotes at Charlie. 'I'm sorry

I was in such a rush the other day. You must have thought me very rude.'

Charlie thanked her and gratefully pocketed the money.

'So long, Charlie – I mean, Charles!' The man laughed.

The woman slapped the man's arm. 'Jerry! Forgive my husband; he thinks he's real funny. Now, what are you going to do with all this money? Not that it's any of my business, mind.'

'I'm going to enter the end-of-course exhibition that is going to be held in there in a couple of days.' Charlie nodded at the Colosseum.

'Now that is exciting, isn't it, Jerry?' said the woman.

'Good luck with that,' said the man.

'Thank you,' said Charlie.

Hidden amongst the crowd, the two street urchins nudged each other. The one wearing the AS Roma football shirt nodded in the direction of Charlie. The one with the scar on his lip shook his head. 'Not now, Fino. Be patient; it's too busy.'

Tito spat on the floor. 'Okay, brother. But let's keep a close tab on the English.' And as Charlie walked away from the Colosseum and back towards the Roman Forum, Tito and Fino stalked him like two cats in the shadows.

XIV

Angelina stretched out on the warm stone steps of the temple. The gang was in a playful mood and she rolled onto her side and watched as they ran about and dodged under the legs of the tourists strolling amongst the ruins of the old Roman Forum. All of a sudden, Angelina sat up. Was that Adriana and Bobby skipping in and out of the broken columns?

'Hey, you two!'

Adriana and Bobby stopped their game. Angelina sat up. She needed to know more about this Bella from Naples. Marco Del Vecchio was her tomcat, and although she would never admit it to anyone else, she was worried that he was intrigued by this fearsome little tortoiseshell. Of course, she didn't have Angelina's looks; but Marco was a tomcat, after all.

'Hey, Angelina!' said Adriana.

Angelina smiled. She knew that curiosity would get the better of Adriana. 'How are you this fine evening?'

Bobby eyed Angelina with suspicion. He didn't like or trust her. He didn't like or trust her gang. In fact, he didn't like or trust anybody, really. He was a loner, a high-plains drifter, a go-ahead-cat-make-my-day sort of guy.

'Still playing the *Americano*, Bobby?' Angelina quipped.

Bobby skipped up to a higher step.

'Charming.'

'Oh, he doesn't mean to be grumpy,' said Adriana.

'It appears you have a lot of *grumpy* acquaintances, Adriana. Anybody would think that they didn't like me or any of my friends.'

Adriana laughed nervously. 'No, it's not like that; not at all. You know what these street cats are like.'

'It may have escaped your attention, Adriana, but we are all street cats. We may come from different districts, but we are all in this together. Especially now, when we are being squeezed out of the district by Romano and his antics.'

'I know. Isn't it dreadful? The restaurants are all being closed down and soon there won't be enough food to go around. What are we going to do? Marco must have a plan.' Adriana jumped up onto the step.

Angelina leant in close. 'But your little friend, Spanish Bella, she seems to get by. She has a survival instinct. You must have heard the story of how she ended up in Rome?'

Adriana shook her head.

Angelina had her audience. 'Well, Marco told me that back in Naples she killed another cat.'

'No! Don't say that, Angelina. It can't be true.'

'But it is, and it was a tomcat, too. She's a tough one. A *real* street cat.'

Adriana shook her head. 'I don't believe it; that's not Bella.'

'But it is, Adriana. Did you ever wonder why they call her Spanish Bella?'

Adriana shook her head.

Bobby jumped down. 'I heard she escaped from Naples on the back of a lorry… in a box of oranges.'

'Who told you that? And why didn't anybody tell me?' asked Adriana.

'Franco told me.'

'Old *Frenchie* himself? I wouldn't trust anything he says.'

'Now, now, Adriana. I heard that Franco has a soft spot for you!' teased Angelina.

Adriana pulled a face of disgust and stuck out her tongue. 'Yuk! He's just a stupid boy.'

As dusk settled, the tourists disappeared and an eerie silence descended upon the Roman ruins; a quiet interrupted by the padding of paws, the mewling of play-fighting cats and the distant echo of evening traffic as people headed home. Angelina stared out across the Forum. In the distance she could see a black figure dancing through the twilight and leaping across the flagstones of the centuries-old road. As the figure got closer, she could see it was Franco running with great determination. Angelina stood up and looked down. Adriana had taken Bobby aside to question him about Bella.

'Angelina, you've got to hear this. Toni's restaurant has been closed down by Romano. That's the last restaurant in Via della Verita. It was Spanish Bella who got Toni caught.'

Angelina cast an anxious glance over her shoulder and held a paw to her lips, beckoning Franco to silence.

At hearing Franco's voice, Adriana and Bobby had stopped their conversation, and came and stood either side of Angelina. Franco looked from one cat to the other.

'What's the problem, Franco?' said Adriana, her anger rising.

'Cat got your tongue?' snarled Bobby.

'Gatti, please…' Angelina sat down on her haunches. 'Let Franco speak; he clearly has important news. And we're all street cats in this together, right? I mean, the food situation is getting completely out of control if Romano has succeeded in closing down all the restaurants in our district.

Things are going to get dangerous if we have to roam other parts of the city looking for food.'

Adriana and Bobby looked at each other behind Angelina's back. She was right. Things were getting desperate in the old district.

Franco swallowed and looked around as the other cats from Angelina's gang closed in on him. 'Besides, there's more…'

Angelina looked at the crowd that had gathered below her and nodded at Franco to continue.

'Bella was seen coming out of the Torre Argentina Cat Sanctuary this morning.'

The cats gasped as one.

'Oh, no.' Adriana felt as if she was going to be sick.

'It can't be true!' snapped Bobby. 'Franco, you're lying!'

Franco shook his head. 'No, Bobby. I'm not. I saw her there myself. Angelina, did you not see her by the Pantheon this morning?'

Angelina nodded.

'I'd followed her up Via de Torre Argentina and nearly got myself knocked over by that English student who for some reason was running like a madman up Via della Rotonda.

'Please tell me it isn't true,' cried Adriana.

'What isn't true?'

'Marco!' Angelina looked over the heads of the gathering crowd of cats to see Marco Del Vecchio.

'What is this I hear about Toni's restaurant and Torre Argentina, Franco?'

'It's true, Marco. *La Margherita* is shut, with a closure notice stuck to the door. Romano has got his wish and every single restaurant in Via della Verita has closed. In fact, that's every restaurant in the district, except *The Black Rose* in Piazza del Paradiso,' said Franco.

'But we can't solely blame Bella. Why, it was only the other day that I was eating there, too…'

Angelina cast Marco a withering look. 'Really? *Do tell.*'

Marco ignored her. 'But what's this about Torre Argentina?'

Franco explained how that very morning he had seen Bella leaving the confines of the cat sanctuary near Pompey's old theatre and followed her to the Pantheon. Bella hadn't turned down the road towards Via della Verita, which could mean only one thing – she had already been fed.

'This is a disgrace!' shouted Bobby.

'I don't believe it!' cried Adriana.

'I never did trust that Spaniard,' mused Angelina.

'Gatti, please.' Marco jumped up onto the steps of the Temple of Romulus and addressed the crowd.

'Gatti, we all know how it is forbidden to eat at the Torre Argentina Cat Sanctuary unless you are injured or ill. There is no excuse for a healthy cat to take provisions away from their less fortunate brothers and sisters. That is an *infamita*. Now, I don't know how they do things in Naples, but when in Rome you do as us Roman cats do, and there are no exceptions!' Marco looked at Adriana and Bobby. 'No exceptions. You did right, Franco. Ordinarily, it is not good to speak ill of others, for that is also not the old Roman way. But this business at the Torre Argentina is not *good* business. Bella needs to answer for what she has done. Friends, Romans…'

'Get them!'

A clattering of stones interrupted Marco's speech. And all at once there was a cacophony of howling voices and screeching cats.

'Sitting ducks, Tito!'

'You mean sitting cats, Fino, you dummy!'

'Get them!'

The boys laughed and growled like maniacs as they flung their arsenal of rocks and ancient brick at the scarpering cats. They had been watching and waiting and had chosen their moment to perfection. For, as the cats listened to Marco their natural wariness had disappeared, and they were easy prey. Tito and Fino ran down the steps, hurling more stones at the cats – who starburst in every direction as they attempted to avoid the missiles.

Run!

Where?

Here!

There!

Come on!

Pandemonium reigned.

Charlie saw the commotion as he walked down the steps into the Forum proper. He had been sat sketching the view across the Forum up to the Colosseum. He was heady with the success of the day and determined to draw inspiration for his exhibition piece. This new set of sketches was needed to earn the money to buy his canvas and oil paints. As he packed away his pad and pencils in the fading light, what sounded like the screams of a thousand banshees pierced the acrid evening air. Charlie hurtled down the steps.

'Hey! What are you doing?' he cried out after the two boys, who were chasing a gang of cats towards the Temple of Vesta.

'Oh, look who's here, Tito.'

'A sitting duck,' laughed Fino.

The pair spoke in a strong Roman dialect and Charlie didn't understand a word they were saying. 'Leave the cats alone.'

'What, these vermin?' said Tito, reverting to a more recognisable form of Italian.

'Vermin? They are synonymous with Rome. They are the Lions of Rome! Why are you throwing stones at them?' said Charlie.

'Quite a speech, English. What business is it of yours with these cats?' Fino spat at the ground.

Charlie eyed the two rocks that the boy wearing the AS Roma top held in each of his hands. He looked at the coarse features of the one with a scar on his top lip. This other one also held weapons in his clenched fists. Charlie felt vulnerable. A whimper from behind caused him to turn. Lying prostrate on the ground was a black cat. Charlie could see dark fluid flowing from the prostrate body.

'What have you done?' Charlie shouted, as he ran over to the cat. It was lying quite still. Charlie knelt down, trying to detect any signs of life. The body was warm, but it didn't flinch at his touch. Poor thing.

Charlie heard the smash of a glass bottle and the rumble of boots, but his senses were dulled by the cruelty of the act he had just witnessed. Before he knew it, he had been pushed to the floor and hands were slapping at his face and feeling his clothing. Charlie was completely disoriented. What was happening? He was being attacked! He punched out wildly and his right fist connected with something bony that cracked upon impact.

'Mother of Jesus and Mary and Holy Water!' Tito staggered back from the blow, clutching his nose.

Fino was kneeling on Charlie's chest and rummaging through his jacket pockets. 'Treasure!' he shouted, as he waved the bundle of banknotes in Charlie's face.

Charlie grabbed hold of a mass of raven curls and pulled back hard.

'Aargh!' shouted Fino, as he fell backwards, letting go of the money, which flew up into the air.

Charlie scrambled up and snatched at the banknotes as they fell to the ground. Then, all he felt was overwhelming pain as a heavy foot stamped down hard on his outstretched hand. Charlie's head spun and he felt as if he was going to pass out. Now he was in a very vulnerable situation.

'Not so fast, English; you can stick to your British Pounds!' Tito wrenched the money from Charlie's grasp.

Then a woman's voice called out across the Forum.

'Run!' shouted Fino.

'Holy Mary and Joseph...' Tito lifted his foot and sped off in pursuit of his brother.

Charlie got onto his hands and knees. His head was spinning, and his hands ached: one from the blow he had landed, the other from being stamped on. Charlie felt sick. He struggled to his feet and shook his head. The contents of his satchel were strewn across the ground, his sketches were torn, his pencils all snapped, and his watercolour paints ruined. He felt in his jacket pockets – empty, save for the key to his apartment. He felt in his trouser pockets and pulled out a single ten-euro note. Charlie unravelled the banknote, scrunched it up in his fist and swung a wild punch through the air.

The Gattara was bending down over the bloodied, listless black cat.

'Is he okay?' asked Charlie.

The Gattara wrapped the cat in her shawl and stood up carefully, cradling the inert figure.

'I tried to stop them,' said Charlie.

The Gattara lowered her head and walked past him, with the wounded animal held close to her chest.

Charlie felt a hand on his elbow and turned to see the Gattara looking up at him. The tears she cried were silent. The Gattara patted Charlie's arm, nodded her head and walked quietly away.

XV

Charlie sat in the front office of the police station, waiting his turn. A woman stood at the counter, blowing pink bubbles with her gum as she waited for the police officer to return. She stood half-facing Charlie with her elbow on the counter and regarded him with a casual toss of her long, blonde ringlets. She raised her eyebrows. Charlie smiled and quickly looked at the floor, her provocative dress sense and mannerisms a little too intimidating for an eighteen-year-old from Hampshire. The uniformed officer returned, and nonchalantly slid open the reinforced glass.

'No,' said the officer.

'No?' The woman raised her hands palms up. 'What do you mean: No.'

'I said: *No.*' The officer stared back at the woman.

The woman flung her hands wildly, banged her fists on the counter, and spewed forth a torrent of invective that Charlie didn't catch, but by the smirk on the officer's face probably called into question his fatherhood, sanity and other unmentionable things besides.

'No?'

The officer didn't look up and pretended to be absorbed in what was written in the book in front of him. He pointed to the door with his pen.

With a stamp of her foot, and a further stream of abuse directed at the officer and Charlie, the woman barged through the door of the police station and out into the street.

'*Prego.*' The officer ushered Charlie to the counter.

'I've been robbed.'

The officer looked at Charlie with a quizzical expression.

Charlie composed himself and spoke slowly. 'In the Roman Forum, I was robbed by two guys, and I think they killed a cat.'

The officer shook his head and spoke in English, 'I'm sorry...'

'You speak English?'

The officer waved his hand dismissively. 'A little bit, yes.'

'I was robbed in the Forum and they killed a cat.'

'What did they take?'

'About two hundred euros.'

'Bankcards, identity papers?'

'Just cash.'

'Injuries?'

Charlie pointed to his face and held up his hand to show his bruised knuckles.

'Witnesses?'

'The Gattara.'

The officer pulled a face. 'The Gattara?'

'Yes, she took the cat away.'

The officer shook his head. 'The money we can't trace, the Gattara won't talk to police – they never do. These cat women don't trust anybody. What about descriptions?'

'They were both about my age, one had a scar, the other black hair – curly, I think – and one was wearing a football top…'

The officer held up his hands. 'Wait, my English is not that good. You'll have to slow down…'

Charlie looked at the officer's name badge: RAPHAEL, like the High Renaissance painter - ironic. 'Wait, I'll sketch them for you.' Charlie reached into his satchel and took out a pad and pencil. He sketched quickly. The officer leant over the counter and watched with great interest as Charlie drew his pencil across the page. Within a matter of minutes, he had produced a perfect portrait of his attackers.

Charlie handed the page over the counter.

The officer looked intently at the images. 'You say these two guys robbed you?'

'Yes, they were stoning the cats. I tried to stop them, and they turned on me. They pinned me to the floor and that one' – Charlie pointed at one of the images – 'he went through my pockets and stole my money. The Gattara scared them off.'

'I think I recognise these guys,' the officer said in English. Then, he looked over Charlie's shoulder and spoke in Italian. 'What do you think, boss? These two here, there's been a number of reports of cats being stoned and tourists being robbed.'

Romano reached over Charlie and snatched the page from the counter. He studied the perfect likeness of both of his nephews and drew a deep breath. Time for the old Romano charm to kick in. 'What's this, *English*? You were robbed? In the Forum by these ruffians? This is dreadful. Officer Raphael, I will take personal charge of this investigation...'

The officer looked at Romano, 'Sir?'

'After all, this great city relies on tourists and visitors – students, even, like this young man – and we cannot have these hoodlums attacking people and killing cats. No, this is a very serious matter and I will personally see to it, young man, that it is investigated properly. It will not happen again.' Romano placed a hand on Charlie's shoulder and ushered him out of the station. 'Now, please go home and rest. You have had a horrible experience. Leave this to me, please.'

Charlie was confused by Romano's display of compassion. He glanced over his shoulder and the look on Officer Raphael's face appeared to mirror Charlie's own thoughts. Charlie felt a great hand turn his head in the direction of the doorway.

'Come now, time to go home. Get some rest and leave this matter with me.'

Romano's bulk blocked the entrance back into the police station.

Charlie nodded, a mute thanks, and walked off.

Romano watched until the student had turned the corner. He looked at Charlie's drawing again. *Idiots*, he muttered. This was not a good situation. Romano folded and ripped the drawing into tiny pieces and put them in his trouser pocket.

Across the road, the Gattara watched. She hugged the still-warm body of Franco to her chest and offered both a curse and a prayer up to the darkening sky.

Romano marched back into the station. 'Back to work, Raphael.'

'Shall I file a crime report about this robbery business, boss? I'm sure I recognise the two suspects.'

'No, Raphael, don't you bother. We'll never find the money, and who cares about a stupid cat?'

'But what about the drawing? Shouldn't we circulate it in order to identify the suspects?'

'Officer Raphael, whilst I admire your keenness and determination, may I remind you that I am the superior officer here. I said that I would take personal charge of this investigation. I'll pass the picture on to the detectives. Now get back to minding the front counter – there's a good man.'

Officer Raphael watched the retreating figure of Romano on the internal CCTV system. He watched as Romano made his way along the corridor to his office. Officer Raphael noted the time in his pocketbook and looked up to see a mass of blonde curls.

The pink bubble popped. 'No?'

Officer Raphael shook his head, waved the woman away, and pressed the rewind button on the CCTV system.

XVI

Nico was sat outside the villa on his scooter. Charlie had not been paying attention to the route he was walking. He just wanted to get home; he'd forgotten all about the party. He jogged over to the other side of the street and turned up the collar of his jacket in a vain attempt to avoid being seen.

'Charlie? Hey, where are you going?'

Charlie puffed out his cheeks and looked up into the night sky. It was no use hiding; might as well suck it up. Besides, a party might be just what he needed after everything that had happened today.

'*Ciao*, Nico!' Charlie called out, as he crossed the street.

Nico held up his right hand and fist-bumped.

Charlie grimaced. 'Ow-ow-ow!' That hurt.

'What's the matter?' Nico grabbed hold of Charlie's right hand.

'Ouch!' Charlie shook his head and snatched back his hand.

'What happened? And your face, too…'

'Charlie?' Leonora opened the tall wooden doors and stepped out onto the street. 'What have you done?'

'I haven't done anything. It was done to me. I ran into a little trouble in the Forum.'

Leonora took hold of Charlie's face and inspected it carefully. 'It looks like you ran into one of the Roman columns in the Forum.'

Charlie reached up and took Leonora's hands from his face. 'I'm sorry about earlier at *La Margherita*. Amerigo has a dark sense of humour...'

'Oh, forget that, it was nothing. He's just another crazy old man who's in love with the memory of Maria's mother. There are plenty of them in Via della Verita. But your hands, your face, what happened?'

Nico got off the scooter and patted the seat. Charlie sat down and told them all about the events of the day: how he had found out that Maria's mother had died on the same day as his father, his offer to serve at the restaurant whilst they visited the cemetery, the pictures he had sold to the American couple, and how he had come across the two thugs stoning cats in the Roman Forum and ended up being attacked and losing all his money. 'Just another day in Rome,' he quipped.

'These two boys, tell me what they looked like.' Nico was agitated.

Charlie described the boy with the scar on his top lip and the one with the curly hair and the AS Roma football shirt. 'I drew a picture and gave it to the police. Romano has it.'

Nico and Leonora looked at each other.

'You gave the picture to Romano?' said Nico.

Leonora put a hand on Nico's shoulder to calm him.

'Yes. He said he would take personal charge of the investigation.'

'That man!' Nico flung his hands in the air and stormed off into the villa.

'I think the two boys who robbed you were Romano's nephews,' said Leonora.

'His nephews? No wonder he said he would personally take charge of the investigation.'

'They're a pair of devils. Last week, when Nico was doing his deliveries for his papa, they robbed him of his money. Tito had a knife…'

'A knife!'

'You mustn't say anything, Charlie. I'm the only one who knows. Nico hasn't told anybody else.'

'But he should go to the police.'

'Oh, Charlie, there is much about Rome and Italy you have to learn. How can he go to the police?

Their uncle *is* the police. He's the senior police officer for our district. Trust me, your investigation – it will have been filed at source.' Leonora looked over her shoulder. 'And you want to know what else happened today?'

'What?'

'Romano closed down *La Margherita*. Apparently, that crazy old man Amerigo was caught feeding a cat...'

'Romano, again! He's the devil and nobody can touch him, Charlie.' Nico was back. 'Welcome to Roma!'

'I've got to go and see Maria. I take it she isn't here?'

Leonora and Nico shook their heads and looked at the ground.

'I'll pop over there now,' said Charlie.

'Charlie,' Leonora called after him, 'see if she wants to come to the party, you know - it might do her good...'

Charlie made his way to Via della Verita. *La Margherita* was in darkness, the closure notice illuminated by a street lamp. It was only nine o'clock, but the street was deserted. In the distance he could hear laughter; it appeared to be coming from the direction of Piazza del Paradiso. Suddenly, a light came on in the window above the restaurant awning. Charlie stepped back across the street to see if he could get a view into the room. The window opened and Maria, resting her elbows on the window sill, looked out into the street.

Charlie walked out of the shadows. He opened his mouth to call out to Maria…

'O Romeo, Romeo, where for art thou?' Amerigo was sat in his usual chair. 'You're in the wrong city, English. All, that lovey-dovey Shakespeare stuff is from Verona, not Rome. Now just get on with it and kiss her. You know you want to.'

'Stop it! Amerigo, you're so embarrassing…' said Maria, 'besides, Rome is a very romantic city.'

'I was just saying that he ought to get on with things,' said Amerigo.

'Do you fancy walking?' said Charlie.

'Walking, where?' said Maria.

'Anywhere,' said Charlie.

'He means *kissing*,' cackled Amerigo.

'I mean walking and talking a little…,' said Charlie.

'Walking, talking, a little *kissing* – but I doubt she'd kiss you with a face like that.'

'Maria leaned out of the window and looked at Charlie. 'What *have* you done to your face?'

'It's a long story, but it's my hands that really hurt,' Charlie held up his battered hands.

'Oh, my God, wait there. I'll be down in a minute. I've just got to check on Papa…' Maria closed the window and the bedroom light clicked off.

'That Romano is something else, is he not? I'll never forgive myself. It's my fault this happened…'

'I wouldn't blame yourself, Amerigo,' said Charlie. 'He was waiting for any excuse, and what better day to do it.'

'This is true. He has the cunning of the devil.'

'So, I've heard.'

Maria came out into the street. 'Papa's asleep. Now, Amerigo, are you going home or sleeping here tonight?'

'May I? I don't think my old legs will make it after all that's happened today.'

Maria gave Charlie a knowing smile as she handed Amerigo the key. 'Go on in and lock up behind you, but leave the back door on the latch so I can get in.'

'Yes, yes… I know. Thank you, Maria. *Buonanotte*, young lovers!'

Maria shook her head and laughed. 'Good night, Amerigo. Now, Charlie… would you like to tell me why you look like you've been hit by a London bus?'

As they walked through the night, Charlie told Maria all about what had happened in the Roman

Forum, and afterwards at the police station. She in turn told him more about Romano and his long-standing vendetta against her father. Apparently, it had all started the day after he had come back to the district as the newly appointed Police Chief. Romano had been away for many years, for when he first joined the police, he had been given a station on the outskirts of Rome. Then, one day, he returned and the shy – almost mute – boy had turned into this loud, bullying policeman. On his first day, he brought her mother flowers, and from then on bombarded her with gifts and cards. He was totally insensitive to her father's feelings and didn't seem to care what anybody thought. Then her mother had told him to stop buying her things, and that's when the trouble started. Next, Romano had found this centuries-old by-law about business owners not being allowed to feed the street cats, and he began closing down all the bars and restaurants. Any excuse, and the closure notices were served. Maria had lost count of the number of restaurants that had been forced out of business. This was why her mother had gone out on the night she died: to speak to Romano and make him see sense. To tell him that if he continued, the whole district would be bankrupt, and no tourists would visit the area. But she never returned that night and Romano's anger at her death – Maria could only assume that it was his obsession with her mother that caused him to become so bitter and twisted – only served to fuel his campaign against the local restaurant owners. All except one eating place in Piazza del Paradiso, *La Rosa Nera*, named after the last film that had starred Valeria Viola: *The Black Rose*. It was the last in the trilogy of films where her mother had played the part of a pirate in the old town of Naples. Maria laughed. 'An old pirate, complete with a claw hand. Ironic, don't you think?'

But Charlie didn't answer – he just let Maria talk.

'And everybody knows that *The Black Rose* is run by Romano's sister; but, what can they do about it? He is the police, he is the law, he rules with an iron fist. If anybody complained, it would be useless; and so, it continues on and on until now. The only restaurant left in the district is in Piazza del Paradiso. Romano has won he has come back to the district, seen his opportunity and then conquered. Romano, just like his name – man of Rome.'

There was a lot that Charlie needed to learn about the Eternal City; it wasn't all castles, lights, priests, and pretty girls.

Present company excepted…. thought Charlie.

They had some distance and had stopped on the ancient Ponte Sant'Angelo, a bridge built by

Emperor Hadrian across the River Tiber, leading to his imposing family mausoleum. Maria was looking down into the muddy waters of the river. Charlie looked all around. It was like a sepia photograph come to life: the yellowed dome of St Peter's Basilica in the background and the angel statues leading the way to the old emperor's resting place. Charlie looked at Maria's profile and felt that same shiver of electricity course through him.

Charlie thoughts escaped. 'I've a lot to learn about this place. It's not all castles, lights, priests, and pretty girls. Present company excepted.'

Maria wrinkled her nose. 'Another joke, Charlie?'

Charlie leaned in towards Maria. Then he hesitated. She giggled and looked away. Charlie wanted to kiss her. He could hear old Amerigo's voice: 'Go on, kiss the girl!' But what if he broke the spell? Charlie had kissed loads of girls. But none of the kisses meant anything. This would be like kissing an angel. Charlie could feel his legs begin to shake. What was it about this girl? Was it her? Was it Rome? Was it…

Get them!

Maria and Charlie turned. Running directly towards them from the far side of the river were Tito and Fino.

'Romano's nephews!' cried Maria.

Charlie reached out to Maria and made to run. But then he saw the cats sat on the pavement in the middle of the bridge. Tito and Fino had not seen Charlie and Maria; they were after the cats. Charlie saw that the cats were too consumed in whatever they were doing to have noticed. In the middle of the group was the little tortoiseshell. It looked as if the other cats were rounding on her, but she was giving as good as she was getting, and the other cats were backing off.

Then the horrific din of scooter engines gunned across the bridge.

'Out of the way!'

Charlie dragged Maria onto the pavement as Nico and Leonora went speeding past at the head of a gang of youths on mopeds and scooters. There was no mistaking their intention: to get to the other side of the bridge and to Tito and Fino. The cats ran about in wild circles; some scarpered past Charlie and Maria towards the sanctuary of the opposite bank, while others jumped on the wall of the bridge. The braver ones just sat in the middle of the road and watched the scooters over their shoulders, ready to run at any second.

Blue lights and the two-tone horn of a police car.

The scooters stopped.

Romano alighted from the police vehicle.

'You two!' he shouted at Tito and Fino. 'Get in here! You lot, back home!'

The scooters stood their ground.

'I'm warning you!'

'Don't move!' shouted Nico.

The scooter riders stood firm.

'Brave in your gang, young Nico. We'll see about that.'

'Go to hell, Romano! This isn't your district. You have no authority here. Besides, where's your back-up?'

Romano walked back to the car and reached in for the radio mike. He stood with one arm on the driver's door and pretended to depress the call button: 'Controller? Yes, this is Police Chief Romano. I am outside the Castel Sant'Angelo. There is a problem with a gang of scooter thugs...'

Nico signalled for the scooters to turn and head back across the river.

'Controller cancel any back-up. They've gone.' Romano placed the radio mike back in its cradle. Once the scooter riders had disappeared, he got back into the car and spoke slowly. 'What did I tell you about chasing and stoning cats? You pair of fools. What happened at the Forum? You think I don't know. You fools! This is going to prove difficult for old Romano, but when the going gets tough and all that... I don't want you two venturing outside of the Piazza del Paradiso for a month – do you hear?'

Tito and Fino looked at the contorted face of their uncle in the rear-view mirror and shrunk back in their seats.

In the meantime, Charlie was running back across the bridge and down the steps that led to the riverbank.

Maria shouted frantically: 'No Charlie!'

But it was too late, and before she could call out again, Charlie had dived into the brown waters of the River Tiber.

XVII

I'm walking pretty,
Through the streets of the Eternal City
Wherever I roam, every street's my home
When I'm roaming in Rome

I'm singing to myself as I walk across the Pont Sant'Angelo, having mooched about the area around the Vatican - the one place in the city that I haven't managed to gain access to - when suddenly I find my path blocked by Marco Del Vecchio and his gang. But it's strange because Angelina is here, and Adriana. It's like, why are the girls here? And Bobby, too.

What's going on?

'What have you got to be so happy about?' says Adriana.

'She has no conscience. That's the trouble with these Neapolitans,' says Bobby.

These two are supposed to be my friends. 'What are you guys talking about? I'm just here, roaming in Rome, minding my own business, and I get all this abuse.'

Adriana is crying. 'It's Franco…'

'He's dead!' Bobby hops up onto the wall of the bridge.

I say, 'What do you mean, Franco's dead?' I'm not getting this at all. What has happened? I'd only been gone one afternoon, but in that short space of time it would appear that something dreadful might have happened.

'Now hang on guys,' says Marco. 'Bella doesn't know about Franco. She wasn't there, so you cannot attach any blame to her for that.'

Thank God for Marco; otherwise I think I may have been lynched. Some of the *gatti* are getting themselves properly worked up.

'But there are still some matters we need to clear up, Bella,' Angelina says.

I wondered when she was going to pipe up.

'Matters?'

'Matters. Such as the fact you were seen being fed by that old man outside Toni's place this afternoon by Romano, who then closed the place down. That's it, Bella: Via della Verita is lost to all of us now.'

'But you can't blame all the closures in Via della Verita on me,' I say.

'This is true,' says Marco. 'Romano started his work a long time before you turned up.'

'And it was only a small piece of ham that Amerigo fed me…'

'Just an itty-bitty, small piece of ham,' mocks Adriana.

I swear I'm going to scratch her eyes out.

'That's enough, Adriana,' says Angelina. I'm warming to this kitty, and she appears slightly more amenable when Marco is around.

'I was hungry. I hadn't had anything to eat all morning.'

'It was Franco who saw you outside *La Margherita*. He'd been following you… from the Torre Argentina Cat Sanctuary.'

Marco's words set alarm bells ringing. The Torre Argentina Cat Sanctuary is the one place that you are not allowed to go, no matter how tired and hungry you get. Only the sick and injured are permitted. It's an unwritten law amongst the cats of Rome. There is no excuse. It is absolute. If you violate this law, it means trouble. The only time you can go to Torre Argentina is if you are taken there by one of the *gattare*, the cat women.

'Hang on,' I say, scrambling in my brain for the information. 'The thing is, I woke up in the early hours of yesterday morning and was chased by this madman. I'd found a garage in a backstreet near to the Piazza del Paradiso, and inside the garage was an old car. It had its window open and on the back seat was this scarf – a fine silk scarf… oh, Angelina, you would know the luxury of such a thing…'

Angelina nods approvingly.

I continue, 'I fell asleep and when I woke up there was this mad, eye-bulging, great ugly face screaming at me in the mirror – it was a man sat in the front seat. He was crying and laughing and shouting, proper crazy-like. I leapt out of the small window at the back and he chased me about the garage, throwing things at me, and the scarf got caught around my neck and legs, and by the time I managed to squeeze through the door and out into the street, I was completely bound. But the Gattara was there. And then the man was gone; it was like the Gattara had this power over him and he just backed off. My heart was thumping so fast and my head ached. Well, the Gattara took me to Torre Argentina. I woke up in a basket – but I swear that as soon as I woke, I left. I didn't take any food, only a little water. That's the true story.'

'Who was the man in the mirror?' says Marco, straight to the point.

'I don't know. I just woke up from a bad dream and I just saw his bulbous eyes.'

Marco nods. He walks over to a small group, clearly his top boys: all black fur and white socks. I don't remember seeing them before. Marco turns back to me. 'Okay, is everyone satisfied with

Bella's explanation?' There is a general murmuring of assent amongst the group.

Adriana creeps over. 'I'm sorry, Bella, it's just that it's so awful what has happened to Franco…'

Adriana and Bobby tell me how they had gone to the Roman Forum and met up with Angelina and her posse. Franco had come to tell them that Romano had closed down *La Margherita* after seeing Amerigo feed me. I admit culpability, but in my defence say that I was incredibly hungry, especially after the events in the garage. I don't tell them about the small plate of pasta the Gattara had left in my crate at the cat sanctuary. I mean, it was only a small plate, and it had been a harrowing experience… Angelina tells me about the two thugs who had been throwing stones earlier at Via della Verita and had then followed them to the Forum. Franco had been hit by a great rock and there was blood everywhere. If it hadn't been for the English boy and the Gattara, they'd have all been killed by the two thugs.

'Where is Franco now?'

'He's dead!' cries Adriana.

'We don't know that, Adriana,' says Marco.

'But the blood!' says Bobby.

Get them!

Before Marco can respond, cats go running in all directions.

Marco stands defiant. 'Tito and Fino, again!'

And then there's a noise that sounds like a swarm of gigantic bees rushing past, and there's all this shouting and blue lights and sirens, and it's like I'm back in Naples.

Look out!

A scooter is speeding along the pavement. It just misses a canoodling couple and heads directly at me. I jump, and I'm falling down through the air.

Falling down into the rushing brown waters of the River Tiber.

XVIII

Charlie ran as fast as he could down the steep steps. He had already seen one cat critically injured today, and he wasn't going to allow another animal to suffer. Charlie found himself scanning the rushing water for any sign of the tortoiseshell cat. He was sure he had seen her jump. Charlie looked up at the bridge. Maria was waving and calling out to him, but the sound of the water drowned out her pleas. He looked at the concrete base of the bridge pillars to see if the cat had fallen there. Charlie paced up and down the embankment, frantically scanning the murky waters for any sign of life.

There!

There she was - spinning in wild, exaggerated circles about ten yards from the bank. Charlie threw off his leather jacket and hopped out of his trainers.

'No, Charlie!' Maria called out, as she ran down the steps, only to watch helplessly as Charlie dived into the foaming torrent.

'Come on, Maria!' Nico had leapt ahead of her and was racing along the bank.

Maria gave chase.

Charlie was swimming with great determination towards the lifeless figure being tossed about by the swirling waters. As he reached her, Charlie grabbed hold of the cat by the scruff of the neck. She was unconscious. At least, that's what he hoped. There was no way she could have drowned in the short space of time that she had been in the water. It wasn't as if it was that cold. But perhaps it was the adrenalin rush that was keeping him warm. Charlie took a great breath and kicked towards the bank, it was too high for him to get out where he had dived in. He hadn't stopped to think things through; but he could make out Nico waving him towards safety. Maria was running past Nico. Where was she going? Charlie saw a pontoon about twenty-five yards to his left. Holding the cat up out of the water with his left hand, he performed a lop-sided breaststroke with his right arm, kicking his legs out in the classic frog-legged fashion. The life-saving course at the local swimming pool hadn't quite prepared him for this. He turned onto his back and placed the cat on his chest, holding her steady with his weaker left hand. He had the crazy notion that his fast-beating heart would somehow shock the cat back to life. But as he kicked his legs and pulled at the water with his free hand, he realised he couldn't see where he was going.

Charlie!

He was getting tired and the voices calling disoriented him. Where were they coming from? Charlie flipped back onto his front, holding the cat by the scruff of her neck again, high out of the water. Incredibly, he was only about five yards from the pontoon.

Nico was clapping his hands. 'Here, here… throw the cat, Charlie!'

Charlie lifted his hand high out of the water and tossed the sodden animal at Nico. The jolting movement caused Charlie's head to go under and he was left coughing and spluttering as the treacly river water forced itself down his throat.

Charlie!

Maria was at the pontoon. She was holding on to a mooring pole with her left hand and reaching out to him. Charlie reached out to grab at Maria, and his hand slipped down her right forearm and off her wrist. The water seemed to want to drag him back out into the middle of the river. But Charlie was a strong swimmer, and he struck out back towards the pontoon.

Maria's face wore a look of panic and frustration. Leonora came up behind her and grabbed the back of her jeans with one hand and held onto the mooring pole with the other. Maria let go and held both her arms out. Charlie reached up and grasped Maria's right arm with both hands. He looked at her face, smiled and nodded reassuringly. Maria took a hold of Charlie's hair with her left hand and pulled – hard!

Like a landed fish, Charlie flopped up onto the wooden pontoon boards.

'Have I got any hair left?' he panted.

Maria fell to her knees and buried her face in his chest.

Leonora knelt down next to her old friend and they embraced.

Charlie couldn't tell if they were laughing or crying.

Nico walked onto the pontoon. They all stared at him. Nico looked up from the prostrate figure he cradled in his arms and shook his head.

XIX

I remember looking up and seeing angels, lots of angels; they were all standing on the bridge, looking down at me. As I hit the water, every gram of strength was expelled from my body and I was swallowed up into the dark depths. The angels shone in the night sky and I thought of Bruno. This was how it was going to end for me, too. I was going to drown. *Quid pro quo*. It was fate; how else could it possibly end? The angels stared and pointed to the heavens as the water swirled above me. I thought of Franco. I thought of Toni. I thought of pizza. I thought of Naples. I thought of the couple canoodling on the bridge, and I thought of Rome. Then I thought: *I can't swim*. My legs are completely still. I'm paralysed. It is only my mind that is raging against the torrent. Do you know that Roma spelt backwards is *Amor*, which is the Latin word for love? *Roma e Amore*. Rome and Love. The canoodling couple looks down at the water. I can see the panic on the boy's face, and I see the girl with the velvet blue eyes. I now know where I have seen their beautiful familiar faces before. *Roma e Amore*.

'She's breathing! Quick, Maria, get my coat!' shouted Charlie.

'Here, take this.' Leonora took off her jumper and held it out for Charlie, who wrapped Bella in the warmth of the merino wool.

They all stared at the small brown, black and gold head.

Bella sneezed.

'There! She's alive! Charlie, you saved her.' Maria held onto Charlie's arm and smiled at the little bundle.

'Come on,' said Nico. 'Let's get you guys back home.'

'You take Charlie back, Nico, and I'll get a cab for Maria and myself.' Leonora looped her arm in Maria's. 'Come on, we've got some catching up to do. Besides, I need your coat – I'm freezing.'

Maria realised that Leonora was stood wearing only a bra on her top half. Nico blushed. They had all been so consumed with Charlie and the cat that they hadn't noticed. Maria laughed. Leonora stood with hands on hips and raised her eyebrows at Nico, who duly averted his gaze.

'Come on, Charlie. Give the cat to the girls,' said Nico, 'and mind you sit well back on the seat of my scooter. I don't want to get my clothes wet!'

XX

Charlie got the small wood-burning stove going. He didn't have any wood, but he had plenty of paper and cardboard pizza boxes. He changed into some dry jeans and hung his wet clothes on the balcony railing. Looking down into the street he saw Maria getting out of the taxi. Leonora waved up him. Charlie blew a kiss. He had left the entrance open and watched as Maria exchanged air-kisses with Leonora before making her way up. It was amazing how the events of the day had brought them all to this. Perhaps all the bad stuff was meant to be.

Maria came into the room carrying the small bundle. 'She's a bit more awake, but I haven't felt her move yet. I don't know if it's the cold, shock, or something worse. It's too late to take her to the Torre Argentina, and there's no guarantee they will have a vet on call. Oh, good, you've got the stove going.' Maria looked around at the general mess that was Charlie's studio and frowned. 'Empty that crate, Charlie... and have you got a *dry* towel?'

Charlie took his paints and brushes out of the wooden crate that he had got from the market. There was still some paper wrappers in the crate emblazoned with the legend: *Producto de Valencia.* Charlie crumpled the papers and threw them into the fire. The smell of burned orange wafted from the stove.

Maria carefully took Bella from Leonora's damp jumper and placed her on top of the towel which Charlie had fetched from the bathroom and placed in the crate.

'Look, she's sniffing at the fire. She's moving her head now. Poor thing.' Maria was knelt on the floor, stroking Bella's arms and legs.

'Do you think she'll be okay?' said Charlie.

'I don't know. I'll come around first thing in the morning when I do the market run…' Maria put her hand over her eyes.

Charlie was down on his haunches, and he put his arms around her quivering shoulders. 'Hey, it'll be okay.'

'The restaurant is all we have.'

'Trust me, it'll be okay. Put it this way, things can't get any worse.'

Maria wiped at her eyes with her hand and laughed. 'Is that what they call the British stiff upper lip?'

'No, it's just a feeling I've got. It's this cat: I keep seeing her around. I think she's lucky.'

'She's not black.'

Charlie mind raced back to the black cat at the Forum, he hadn't been so lucky. 'Well, she's sort of a bit black... and brown, and orange...'

Maria looked into the crate, and then she leant in closer. 'Hang on, I know this cat. This is the cat that Papa calls the Mozzarella Bella...'

Charlie nodded.

At the mention of her name, Bella mewed.

'Oh, my God!' Maria's hand went to her mouth. 'It's her; it's the cat Papa feeds pizza. He swears this cat can understand him, and he says she comes from Napoli...'

Bella mewed.

Maria stood up. 'This *is* the Mozzarella Bella. I think you might be right, Charlie. If she pulls through, it's an omen. Now, make sure you shut the stove door so the fire burns slowly, and get some sleep. I'll see you in the morning. Perhaps we can tidy up your room a little – what do you think? *Notte.*'

'Good night...' and before Charlie had a chance to say any more, she was gone.

Charlie went to the balcony and watched as Maria walked across the Piazza della Rotonda.

Turn around, he whispered to himself. Just as she passed the fountain, Maria turned. That smile was enough to tell him. He looked over his shoulder at the little cat snuggling in the orange crate.

Charlie laughed to himself: 'Mozzarella Bella and the English Fella – it sort of has a ring to it! What do you think?'

Bella mewed, settled herself in the warmth of the crate and slept.

Day 5

Angel with the Cross - *Ponte Sant'Angelo*

XXI

Charlie looked at the cracks in the ceiling. It was unusually quiet in his studio. The faint, muffled sounds of the Piazza della Rotonda crept in through the gaps in the closed window shutters that allowed a little light to enter the room. Charlie's arms and legs ached. It must have been the shock of all yesterday's events, as well as the physical exertion of rescuing Bella, that caused his body to feel so numb. He felt the warmth of the sleeping body nestled against his legs. Despite the assault in the Forum and the loss of all his money, there was plenty to smile about: for a start, he had been able to get really close to Maria, who in turn had made up with Leonora; and they'd all saved the Mozzarella Bella. Then, Charlie remembered that *La Margherita* had been closed by Police Chief Romano, and he had no money to enter the end-of-course exhibition. His inner smile faded. He shut his eyes and let his hand creep down to touch the warm furry bundle that had taken up residence on his duvet. Charlie looked up at Bella, who was sat on her haunches, ready to pounce from her position on the chest of drawers next to the bed.

Charlie jumped up and stood on top of his bed, pressing himself hard up against the wall.

The rat stared up at him: nose sniffing, whiskers twitching.

Bella let loose a noise that seemed to go from a whisper to a scream in a micro-second, and then she pounced.

All hell broke loose.

The noise was sickening: the frantic effort of the rat trying to find purchase as its feet scratched at the marble-tiled floor in a desperate bid to escape; the thud and scrape as the animals bounced off walls and furniture, crashed through cups and plates, smashed into paint pots and brushes, and upset all of his work. Charlie watched helplessly as the cat and the rat whirled in a crazed *Tarantella*. The rat kept running in mad circles as it dodged each swipe of the cat's paws. Bella couldn't help herself skidding across the wet floor as the spilt paints and water converged to form a multi-coloured lake that transformed into a darker shade of blue, before eventually turning black.

Charlie threw a pillow as the protagonists stood eye-to-eye, a brief pause in the fighting as they took an opportunity to catch their breath.

The pillow landed with a dull thud at least four yards wide of the intended targets. Neither the cat nor the rat averted their gaze. Then, Bella's back legs began to twitch as she prepared to hurl herself into the fray once again. The rat's nose trembled furiously as it frantically sought an escape route. The deadly dancers were set to duel again.

Charlie spotted his chance.

He jumped from the bed and ran to the windows and flung them open; he unclipped the brass lock on the wooden shutters and pushed. The bang of the shutters hitting the outside wall caused Maria to look up to the balcony. She could hear Charlie shouting and the stifled screams of the tourists as heads turned upwards.

The rat looked down from the railings. It looked back quickly and then flung itself towards the ground as Bella dashed out onto the balcony. A quick glance, a slight adjustment of her feet and the tortoiseshell cat was hurtling towards the cobbled pavement. The tourists jumped out of the way. Bella hit the ground running in hot pursuit of her prey. Pedestrians stood back, cyclists braked, scooter riders swerved, and horse carts were pulled to an abrupt halt to avoid collision. The Piazza della Rotonda came to a standstill as the chase continued through the market stalls and under restaurant tables.

Maria looked towards the Pantheon. A group of cats were on the move.

Angelina and her posse, which included Adriana and Bobby, had seen the commotion. They had followed Bella's pursuit with keen interest and now it was time to join in the hunt.

Maria looked up at Charlie, who stood on the balcony. 'What happened?'

Charlie threw his hands up. 'I woke up stroking a rat!'

'What?'

'I thought it was Bella, but when I looked, she was on the chest of drawers ready to pounce.'

'I can't leave you alone for five minutes without you causing trouble, Charlie!' Maria laughed and held up the paper bag she was holding. 'Breakfast to go?'

Charlie gazed down at Maria and the lines from his GCSE English Literature studies came flooding back:

Two of the fairest stars in all of heaven,
Having some business, do entreat her eyes
To twinkle in their spheres till they return…

Shakespeare: *Romeo and Juliet*, only it was the girl who was looking up at him – the balcony scene in reverse. Charlie shook his head and waved her up.

'Are you okay?'

Charlie nodded as he took a pastry from the bag that Maria had placed on the table, and a paper cup of espresso that she held out to him.

'What a mess!' Maria said, as she removed the lid from her own cup and blew on her coffee. 'Well, a bigger mess than it already was.'

Charlie looked about the apartment. It was the first chance he'd had to survey the damage caused. 'Everything's ruined. Every single picture I drew yesterday afternoon at the Forum has been trashed by Tito and Fino; all I have left are just rough sketches and doodles. My paints are upset, and my pencils broken. That's it, Maria, I'm finished. I can't possibly get the money to enter the end-of-course exhibition now. I might as well pack up and go back to England.'

Maria surveyed the wreckage. Charlie's torn pictures had been scattered across the floor and lay amongst the broken pots and spilled paint.

Charlie sat down on the bed and put his head in his hands.

'Where's that stiff upper lip gone, Charlie? Let's have a look at these doodles.' Maria touched his shoulder and then walked amongst the clutter. She put her coffee cup down on the table and picked up the pictures one by one and carefully shook the excess water from the paper. Charlie watched as Maria laid the drawings out on the table. After careful scrutiny, she pushed the pictures that had been completely torn and obliterated to one side. There were six sketches that had survived mostly intact. They were all spoiled by the black imprint of a cat's paw prints trailing across the page, partially obscuring the perfect landscape images of the Roman Forum and the Colosseum as drawn by Charlie. Maria bent down to the ground and searched amongst the various brushes and pencils until she found a black drawing pen. Charlie sat watching, fascinated at the concentrated look on Maria's face. What was she doing?

Maria held up her left hand. 'You sit there and wait.'

Charlie sat back down as he'd been told and finished his breakfast. Eventually, he broke the silence. 'Good pastry…,' he ventured. But Maria was working the pen across one of the papers on the table. 'Great coffee, too… did you make it?'

'The coffee or the pastry?'

'Both.'

'No.'

Maria was leaning into the page and moving the pen in small circles.

'Where did you get them?'

'Is this what you call small talk, Charlie?' All the time Maria was focused on what she was doing.

'Just asking.' If only he could see what she was doing; but every time he moved to take a look, Maria fixed him with a stare and raised the stump of her right wrist to stop him in his tracks.

'Charlie – sit!'

'Sorry; curious, that's all.'

'You know what they say about curiosity?'

'I do, and I wish that I'd left that cat to drown now.'

'Charlie, how could you say that? I know you don't mean it, really.'

Of course, he didn't mean it. But he couldn't help but think that if that darned cat hadn't come back to the apartment, everything would have been all right. Okay, he would have been up against it, but he might have been able to sell some pictures today.

'Besides, that cat is going to make you a small fortune. At least we're going to get that money you need to enter the exhibition. Come, look at these.'

Charlie got up and stood behind Maria.

He couldn't believe it.

What had she done to his drawing?

'Do you like it?' Maria looked up him, the girl with the stars in her eyes.

Charlie swallowed.

'You don't like it?' Maria sounded downcast.

Charlie wrapped his arms around her and squeezed hard, causing Maria to yelp as she spilled her coffee.

'I love it. But what are you doing to me? I'm supposed to be a serious artist.'

'And a poor one, too. Now, sit down and let's get to work on the others.'

Charlie looked at what Maria had drawn and copied the design onto the sketch he had in front of him. Before long, they had completed the six pictures between them. Imagine this: pencil drawings of Rome landscapes with the imprint of cat's paws wandering across the page; now add a silhouette of a black cat... and sign off the picture: *Charli Gatti.*

'There you go, Charlie. Six original drawings; all we have to do now is sell a few copies of the *Charlie Cats.*'

'Maria, we have *six* pictures. If I'm to earn the money to enter the competition and buy a large canvas and new paints – it may have escaped your notice, but I don't have any materials left – then each of these pictures is going to have to sell for about fifty euros.'

Maria tilted her head to one side and inspected the pictures. 'I wouldn't pay fifty euros for one of them. In fact, I probably wouldn't give you fifty euros for the lot.'

'Thanks. So, what do you suggest?'

'*Elementare, mio caro Charlie.*'

'Is that supposed to be a joke?'

'No, not a joke. I've got it all sorted.'

Maria picked up the pictures and carefully placed them in Charlie's portfolio, before making her way to the door. 'Shall I wait for you downstairs?'

'Aren't I coming with you, now?'

'Not until you've had a shower – you still smell of the Tiber! I'll see you outside in ten minutes,' and Maria flashed the fingers of her left hand, twice. 'No, make it twenty, or maybe thirty – you need a decent wash.'

Charlie shook his head and laughed. She was like a whirlwind. He had never met anybody so focused. No fuss, no nonsense, straight to it. Amerigo was right: Maria was beautiful and hard-working. She was also a right bossy so-and-so. Charlie walked to the bathroom, jumped in the shower and thought about the girl with stars in her eyes.

XXII

I'm running down Via de Torre Argentina, chasing after the rat. He's quick, I'll give him that. And I have to keep a careful eye on him as he dodges – this way and that – in a vain attempt to shake me off. But I'll keep running, because nobody gate-crashes my party. The boy saved me, and I owe him this much. Besides, I haven't had much opportunity for rat-catching recently, as the streets around the Via della Verita are surprisingly free of rodents. Then, I'm running as part of a gang. It's like I'm back on the streets of Naples and this is our very own feline world of adventure.

'Feeling better?' says Angelina. She's as quick as she is pretty. 'Good to have you back. Where did the rat come from?'

'Piazza della Rotonda, the boy's apartment…' I'm panting hard, but feeling good, nonetheless.

'It's okay, Bella, you deserved a warm bed last night,' smiles Angelina. 'Come on, guys, let's show this rodent what we're about.'

I'm surrounded by cats: Angelina, Adriana, Bobby, and the rest of the crew. I turn to my right and the handsome face of Marco Del Vecchio is set fierce in concentration.

'I reckon he's heading towards Piazza del Paradiso,' shouts Marco. 'But it means crossing the *Corso* – who's with me?'

'This is a very strange business, boss,' says one of the white-socks. 'We're all with you!'

Before I know it, we are all running amongst the braking cars and buses as we cross the busy *Corso*. It's chaos. Amazingly, no-one gets hurt. But what chance does the morning traffic have when a wild gang of street cats decide they're crossing the *Corso*?

Bobby shouts, 'Gatti – look!'

And I'm chasing with Marco Del Vecchio and his boys as rats come running out of every hole in the Piazza del Paradiso.

'They're everywhere!' shouts Adriana.

'Now we know where they've been hiding,' says Bobby, and I can tell that he feels like a cowboy in a Western movie, galloping after the herd.

There must be at least two hundred rats and twenty of us cats. I'll take the ten-to-one odds any time with these guys. I get the feeling like I used to have in Naples that nobody can stop us when we are going about our *business* – there, I'm back in the fold. You can run away, but you cannot hide once a street cat, always a street cat. And that's me, folks:

Sempre una gatta di strada – always a street cat. We run as one and all into the Pizza del Paradiso, and that's where it went totally crazy and became that awful mess of a business.

XXIII

Romano stood with his chest puffed out, self-assured in his own importance. 'Of course, Comandante, if you would like to treat your lovely wife to a wonderful meal, I will personally ensure that you get the best table at *The Black Rose*. It is a delightful restaurant, and one that has listened and paid heed to the local by-laws. As you saw, in the Via della Verita there are no places open for business. This place is a goldmine – the owners are going to clean up.'

The Comandante frowned. 'I'm not certain that I share your enthusiasm for empty streets and failing business, Romano. How is it that this place has managed to escape your watchful eye?'

'But, Comandante, all the business owners were given fair warning. The cats are pests, they are vermin. The tourists would prefer to eat and drink in peace. Look at the customers here at *The Black Rose*, enjoying their cappuccino and breakfast pastries without being disturbed by begging moggies. The Via della Verita could have been like this if the other restaurant owners had listened and not fed the cats.' Romano raised his arms in a resigned manner. 'It is a pity. It's a shame. But what can I do? I'm just a policeman invoking an ancient by-law…'

Rats!

Run!

The Comandante turned at the sound of the screams. Piazza del Paradiso turned into the nine circles of Dante's Hell: the customers of *The Black Rose* fled in all directions; hotel guests disappeared back inside their lobbies; the shopkeepers locked their doors; chairs and tables were strewn across the pavement in panic as the great mischief of rats swarmed into the piazza. The rats ran straight past Romano, who stood helpless, his hands held up high and his police whistle in his mouth, and in through the open door of *The Black Rose* restaurant.

Romano blew on his whistle and yelled: *Stop!*

But the marauding glare of cats ignored the impotent demands of the policeman and stormed into *The Black Rose*. The yowls and screeches were drowned out by the petrified screaming of Romano's sister, Paola, who hurtled out of the premises closely followed by Tito and Fino.

'Uncle – help us!'

'Please, uncle!'

'Brother, please!'

Romano looked aghast.

The Comandante looked from the woman to Tito and Fino, and finally to Romano. What was going on here? Who were these two urchins that called his Police Chief 'Uncle'? Why did that woman refer to him as her brother? The Comandante's investigative brain went into overdrive as the cats emerged from the restaurant as one and took up residence in the now-empty piazza.

'Romano, what is the meaning of this?'

'Comandante, I don't know what you mean. I don't know these people. Well, I know them as citizens of my district - that is all...'

'But, Uncle Romano, why do you say that?' said Tito.

Romano slapped the boy around the face.

'Monster!' shouted Paola. 'You hit your very own flesh and blood.'

'*Pazzo*,' said Romano, pointing to his temple. 'This woman is suffering from shock. She doesn't know what she's talking about.'

It was at that point that Fino walked up and stamped down hard on Romano's foot, causing him to hop wildly until he lost his balance and fell onto the grey cobbled stones.

The Comandante walked up to *The Black Rose*. He reached inside the breast pocket of his jacket and removed the folded sheet of paper.

'No, Comandante, I beg you, please. I will sort this mess out, I promise…,' pleaded Romano, as he struggled to his feet.

The Comandante peeled off the gummed backing sheet and slapped the notice on the restaurant window. He took out his pen and wrote in capital letters:

CLOSED DUE TO RAT INFESTATION!

XXIV

When Charlie walked out onto the street, Maria was waiting.

'Where's my portfolio?'

'Don't worry, it's safe. Come.' Maria looped her right arm through Charlie's left and turned his face towards her with her left hand.

Was this the moment? Charlie had washed and brushed his teeth in anticipation of that first kiss.

Maria inspected him carefully and ruffled his hair. 'Better; you almost look human. Now, on your best behaviour, and none of that serious artist nonsense,' and she pulled him along the road.

The cheek of the girl. Who did she think she was? Charlie wasn't used to being told what to do; he felt himself bristle.

Maria saw the look on his face. 'What's the matter? Don't you want to win that competition?'

'Win it? I'm not even in it. Maria, seriously, how am I going to get the money to pay for everything? The last day for fees is today; entries have to be in by close-of-play tomorrow…'

'What is this *close-of-play*? What does this mean? Is it like the stiff-upper-lip?'

'What? No, nothing like the stiff upper lip. It means I'm running out of time and I haven't painted anything yet. The exhibition is only two days away and…'

'*Elementare, mio caro…*'

'I wish you'd stop saying that.'

Maria looked him in the eyes.

And then she kissed him…

At least, that's what happened in Charlie's head. 'Well?' he said, hopefully.

'We've got work to do,' giggled Maria, as she guided him into the art shop.

'Ah, Maria, see what you think of these…,' said the man, handing Maria a set of postcards.

'What do you think, Charlie?' said Maria, thumbing through the prints. 'Pretty good, eh?'

Charlie took the postcards from Maria. The set of six postcards were prints of the drawings that they had earlier annotated with the cat silhouette and the *Charli Gatti* logo.

'They look amazing.'

'I'll tell you the deal,' the man spoke perfect English. 'I'm going to print a hundred of each postcard. You can have them on credit, and if you sell them all at four euros for a set of six, then you'll have enough to enter the exhibition, buy your materials – from here, of course, for we are an art and print studio – and have enough left over to pay me back. There is one condition, though.'

'What's that?'

'When you see me at the exhibition, you keep our little business arrangement secret.'

Charlie was a little puzzled.

'I'm Signor Roberto, one of the competition judges. I'm a sponsor of the *Accademia*, and this little arrangement is not proper and right at all. But Maria tells me that you can be relied upon to be discreet. Do we have a deal?'

Charlie shook the outstretched hand. 'Deal.'

'You have a great talent; now show me what sort of a businessman you are. Your manager here tells me you need a little educating in this department.'

'My manager… So, when did this happen?'

Maria spoke to the man in the Roman dialect. Charlie didn't understand a word she said. Signor Roberto laughed. 'Just like her mother, a shrewd businesswoman. You'll need to watch this one, young man. Give me an hour.'

'Now, what's all this manager business?' asked Charlie, as Maria ushered him out of the shop.

Maria held up her right arm for silence and spoke into her mobile phone: '*Ciao*, Leonora. Are you free this morning? Yes? What about Nico? And

Patricia? *Bravo*, can you meet Charlie and me outside the art studio in Piazza della Rotonda in about one hour? Excellent. *Ciao-ciao* – bye-bye… There, all sorted. What shall we do in the meantime? How about we take a stroll around the Pantheon and you get some inspiration for your masterpiece?'

Charlie saw the butcher coming towards them. 'Oh, no…'

'No more credit, do you hear? You said you were going to pay me yesterday and instead here you are, bold as brass, canoodling with this girl… Maria? Is that really you?'

'*Buongiorno*, Signor Marcello.' Maria turned to Charlie. 'Another debtor? And I thought you were a rich Englishman – never mind. Signor Marcello, I'll make sure he has your money by close of play this evening.'

The butcher looked confused. 'What is this *close-of-play* business?'

'By five o'clock. You have my word.'

'Ah, Maria, you're a good girl. As for you – no more sausage and no more credit!'

'I've got a feeling he doesn't like me,' said Charlie, as they walked with the throng through the open doors of the Pantheon. 'Besides, I thought he had let me off the money until I could afford to pay.'

'Oh, Signor Marcello is okay… a little forgetful in his old age, but it's not him you need to worry about. It's his eldest son, Francisco; he's been asking me to go out with him for over a year now. You ought to be careful – a jealous Roman butcher's son can be deadly.'

'But why would the butcher's son be jealous?' teased Charlie.

Maria gave a coy smile. 'Well, he might think – you know, that something…'

'That something…'

Maria nudged Charlie with her shoulder. 'You know…'

Charlie looked up through the open dome of the Pantheon and marvelled at how the sun's rays illuminated the interior in glorious golden hues. When he looked down, Maria was staring up at him.

Charlie bent his head down for the first kiss – what a place, right here in the Pantheon. The church of all gods.

But he was kissing air.

Charlie opened his eyes.

Maria grabbed his hand. 'Come on, we've got work to do.'

Nico and Leonora were sat by the fountain in Piazza della Rotonda. Patricia was talking to one of Signor Marcello's sons outside the butcher's shop.

'Is that the one?' whispered Charlie.

'Shush,' laughed Maria, digging him in the ribs.

'Ouch!'

'Deadly weapon,' said Maria, holding up her right wrist.

'So, what have you got planned for us, Maria?' asked Patricia, joining the group.

Maria waved Charlie off in the direction of the art studio whilst she told the others her grand scheme. They all nodded enthusiastically. It sounded like a masterplan. It was agreed. Charlie came back carrying three boxes.

'There you go – six hundred original *Charli Gatti* postcards, all cellophane-wrapped in packs of six. That's one hundred packs at four euros each. If we sell them all, I'll have more than enough money.'

Patricia threw her arms around Charlie. 'He's sold his artistic soul to the devil!'

'Or Maria,' laughed Leonora, and the three girls stood abreast, with their arms around each other; giggling, just like the old days.

Nico picked up his crash helmet and sat astride his scooter. 'Okay, give me the merchandise.'

Charlie handed him a box. 'Thank you, Nico.'

'No problem. I'm getting used to you being around.' Nico whistled at Leonora – who pulled a snappy yes-sir salute – and patted the seat behind him. 'We're off to the Colosseum and the Forum. See you back here in a couple of hours.'

Charlie gave a thumbs-up to Leonora as Nico gunned the scooter engine. Maria hailed a cab and picked up one of the boxes. She and Charlie were going to hit the area around the Campo de' Fiori. Patricia was going to work the Piazza della Rotonda and the streets around the Trevi Fountain.

'I hope you don't mind, but I've enlisted a helping hand,' said Patricia.

'*Chi è?*' asked Maria. 'Who is it?'

Patricia bit her forefinger and indicated with her thumb over her shoulder as the eldest of Signor Marcello's sons walked over to the fountain. 'You know, Francisco…'

'*Ciao*, Francisco. How are you?'

'I'm very well, Maria.' Francisco kissed Maria's cheeks. 'You haven't introduced me to your artist friend.'

'Charlie, meet Francisco… A very old friend of mine; we've known each other since we were at primary school.'

Charlie had taken his seat in the rear of the taxi next to Maria and leaned across to offer his hand. The butcher's son grasped and squeezed. It was like shaking hands with a giant. How did somebody's hands get so big?

'Nice to meet you, Charlie.'

'And you...' Charlie felt his already-bruised fingers being crushed again as Francisco took a firm grip of his hand and kept a keen hold on his eye.

'Shall I take the money for the sausage out of our earnings?' Francisco winked at Maria and released his grip. '*Arrivederci.*'

'Goodbye.' Charlie grimaced.

'Now you're the best of friends with Francisco.'

Charlie shook the life back into his dead hand. 'Bad joke, Maria. Now, get in.'

The taxi took them down to the Corso Vittorio Emanuele II and dropped them off near to the site of Pompey's Theatre, or at least the piazza dedicated to it. There were cats on every street corner. Maria nudged Charlie, who was still nursing his crushed fingers. What was going on? The cats were stood like sentinels.

'It's like they're watching for something,' said Maria, as they entered the market square.

The Campo de' Fiori was in full cry. The market stallholders were shouting, the customers were gesticulating, and the whole place was a riot of noise and colour, and cats...

'Something's happened,' said Maria.

'Look,' said Charlie, pointing. 'Over there by the statue, it's Mozzarella Bella.'

'Charlie, I think the river water has dulled your brain. You're as bad as Papa. There are hundreds of scraggy brown cats in Rome… Oh, my life, you're right!'

'I told you it was her!' Charlie had jumped up onto the concrete plinth of the statue and was tickling Bella under the chin. 'I swear this cat can understand me… *Thank you for saving me from the rat and ruining my pictures...*'

Maria took her phone out and captured the moment. 'Say *cheese…*'

'Who is this bloke?' Charlie pointed up to the statue. 'He looks like a character from *Star Wars.*'

'Funny you should say that. He was a philosopher, mathematician and poet. He believed in the infinity of the universe and pretty much spoke of the Big Bang Theory back in the sixteenth century. He was considered an enemy of the Roman Catholic Church. The Roman Inquisition found him guilty of heresy and he was burned at the stake here on this very spot in 1600. The fact that he was from Naples didn't help.'

'You Neapolitans seem to wind everybody up. What was his name?'

'Bruno, his name was Giordano Bruno…'

'Hey, where are you off to?'

Bella had jumped off the statue and ran over to where Marco Del Vecchio was addressing the gang.

The mention of the name 'Bruno' was ringing in her ears. After the events of last night and that awful mess in the Piazza del Paradiso, her nerves were shredded. And now the canoodling couple, again - and all this talk of Bruno.

'Here comes, Bella.' Angelina nods for me to take the seat next to her as Marco begins to speak.

'I want you all to go out today and spread the word. This business has to stop.'

'What business, boss?'

'This business…'

Business, business, always business… My head is spinning. I'm thinking about the orange crate and the wood burner in the boy's apartment. Wouldn't life be so much easier sitting around all day, lying out on that balcony and just watching the world go by? But, to a street cat, even thinking about such comforts amounts to heresy. Look at how they had reacted when they thought I'd had taken food at the Torre Argentina Cat Sanctuary. It is only the sick and needy that need homes, right? Healthy cats have a job to do on the street.

'I fear that, with all this business of Romano and the closures, we have neglected our brothers and sisters,' continues Marco. I look at the crowd. Brutal faces stare back at me: old faces; young faces; faces that have seen a fight or two; faces that have been around a bit; worldly-wise and ignorant faces. Marco's audience nods as one. 'So, this business, this awful mess in the Piazza del Paradiso, I see as a watershed. From this moment, we take back this city. We will rid the streets of the true vermin who seek to suffer our business. For we are all in this together. This is something that I have learned. Not from a Roman cat, but a Neapolitan cat; indeed, a cat from Naples that we refer to as "The Spaniard"... Bella here has shown me that we shouldn't be fighting amongst ourselves. This business is *stupid* business...'

How many times had he said the word 'business'? I'm struggling to keep up with Marco's speech as he slips in and out of the Roman dialect, but it sounds pretty good, nonetheless.

'No, our true enemies are the rats and the Romano gang. That Police Chief and his tearaway nephews, who inflicted such harm on Franco and closed down all the eating joints. We have Bella to thank for this. If she hadn't chased that rat, we would have all been fighting each other over the scraps in the other districts. It's time to take back the Regalo district; time to take back Navona and the Ghetto. Friends, Romans, cats of Naples and the world: it is time to take back our streets and to do so with the honour and dignity of our ancestors, for we are the Lions of Rome!' The Campo de' Fiori had never heard a din like it. The huge glory of cats sat and yowled as one.

Maria slapped a packet of postcards into Charlie's chest. 'Off to work we go!' She began to shout: 'Charli Gatti! Charli Gatti! Come and get your original postcard images of the Eternal City, signed by the artist himself. You don't believe me? Take a look at the classic pencil work, *raggazi*... see the cat's paws. I could tell you the legend of how the artist jumped into the River Tiber and saved the cat from drowning, and how the cat repaid this act of selfless heroism by stepping into his paints and adding her own signature to his artwork. But you'd never believe me. You'd say: *Really, signorina? Is that the truth?* And I'd have to say: Yes! I swear, upon my Papa's life, as I stand here now, listening to the caterwauling of those street cats on the corner – you see, that one there, the tortoiseshell... yes, it's all her handiwork. *Charli Gatti*! Four euros, *signora. Grazie*! *Charli Gatti*!'

Charlie followed her, carrying the box of postcards, as Maria walked through the crowd, left hand held high, shouting at the top of her voice. She was talking so fast that Charlie could only catch the odd word. What had happened to her? He knew about her work ethic, he had witnessed first-hand her tenacity, but this Maria was so loud and confident, people were drawn to her. The sincerity in her smile and the sparkle in the sapphire-blue eyes had a hypnotic effect on the crowd, and Charlie was dipping into the box and handing over sets of postcards in exchange for the money being thrust towards him. Before long, Maria was stood on an upturned orange crate and regaling the crowd with the story of the *Mozzarella Bella and the English Fella*. The cast of characters grew, and the story got tighter in its retelling. It was just after lunch when Charlie tapped Maria on the shoulder and waved the empty box at the assembled crowd.

'We'll be back with more this afternoon!' shouted Maria.

The people groaned in disappointment.

'Wait there…' An excited murmur went up as Maria talked into her phone. 'Five minutes, ladies and gentlemen, and more supplies will be here. In the meantime, I'll let you in on a secret.' Maria hopped off the crate and waved to the children in the crowd to follow her. 'Remember I told you all about the Mozzarella Bella and the English Fella? Yes?' Maria pointed to the statue of Giordano Bruno, the *Obi-Wan Kenobi* of the Renaissance period.

'Well, there they are, folks. Come on. Only one euro for a personal photo with Bella and Charlie!'

'So now you're pimping me out?' Charlie said, as the first child handed him a coin.

'You love it, Charlie. You always wanted your fame. Well, this is what it looks like in twenty-first century Rome.'

Charlie shook his head and then leaned in next to Bella while the child's mother took a photo of the three of them. The woman then handed him another one-euro coin, sat down next to Charlie, put her arm around his shoulder and took a selfie.

Maria rolled her eyes and shook her head.

'Get used to it, girlfriend. This is how it will always be if you fall in love with the good-looking ones,' said Leonora, unclipping her helmet and shaking her hair loose. 'That's why I've decided to give my heart to Nico.'

'You have?' said Nico, leaning over the handlebars of the scooter.

'Yes, didn't I tell you? I decided last night when you rode like a true Roman warrior straight at those idiots on the Ponte Sant'Angelo. I thought: *that's the one for you, Leonora; you've been blind to his affections all this time – that's the boy for you.* That's what I thought. So, now you know.'

Nico nodded. 'Thanks.'

'You're welcome. Now give me that box of postcards. I want to see this girl in action.'

Nico handed the box to Leonora, who in turn passed it to Maria, who started up her street-trader's banter: '*Charli Gatti! Charli Gatti!* Get your postcards and selfies with the artist right here, right now! There you go! I said there would be more, and I'm a *ragazza* of my word. Who wants a set of postcards *and* their photo taken with the *Mozzarella Bella and the English Fella*?'

Leonora looked at Nico. 'What on earth?' she said, as she looked from Maria to Charlie and then to the cat.

Nico shrugged. 'Don't ask me – she's your friend.'

Within half an hour, Maria had asked Leonora to contact Patricia and tell her to come over to Campo de' Fiori with any postcards she had left over. Truth be told, Patricia had spent more time chatting up Francisco than actually selling the postcards, but it didn't matter, because the desire to be a part of the *Charli Gatti* story in the old street market kept getting stronger. It almost got to the point where Maria was thinking of calling Signor Roberto to print more cards. Then she realised that Charlie needed to get back to his studio and start on his exhibition piece.

By two o'clock, they had done it. One hundred sets of postcards sold and nearly two hundred photos taken. Charlie complained that his face ached. Francisco asked him if his hand was still sore. *Funny*. It was time to head back to the Piazza della Rotonda and a well-earned drink.

Charlie addressed the table: 'I would like to raise a cup of cappuccino…'

'You can tell he's English – fancy drinking cappuccino in the afternoon!' said Leonora.

Charlie looked at his cup.

'You don't drink your coffee with milk after eleven o'clock in the morning. Don't the English know anything?' Nico nonchalantly sipped at his glass of water.

Charlie raised his cup. 'As I was saying, before I was so rudely interrupted…,' and he looked at Leonora under his outstretched arm.

Leonora waved her hands. 'Just saying… I mean, if you want to stay in Rome, you'll have to learn our proper ways.'

'Say, did you hear about what happened in the Piazza del Paradiso earlier today?' said Francisco.

'Somebody said something about rats,' said Nico.

'Yes, a load of cats chased some rats into *The Black Rose* and the Comandante was there when it happened and blamed it all on Romano,' said Francisco.

'What happened to Romano?' asked Maria.

'Apparently, he's been suspended and the Comandante slapped a closure notice on *The Black Rose*.' Francisco appeared to be up-to-speed with all the news.

'No!'

'Yes, and the Comandante lifted the closure notices on *all* the other restaurants in the districts. You should be happy, Maria.' Francisco looked at her intently.

'I should be. But it seems everybody knew that Romano owned a large share in *The Black Rose*, except the police,' said Maria, staring into her drink.

'Who told you that?' asked Francisco.

Maria shrugged her shoulders. 'I just know.'

'You should be careful, Maria. Romano has powerful friends,' warned Francisco.

'What, you mean *ex*-Police Chief Romano? At least that's him out of the way for a while.' Nico banged the table.

'Even more reason to say a huge thank-you and raise our glasses and cups to Maria!' Charlie sensed the mood was getting a bit ugly and thought it best to move on.

The table clapped as one.

Bravo!

'But, first…'

Oh, I thought he was done?

Wait, there's more…

'But first, I would just like to say: Where *did* you learn to sell like that?'

Everybody clapped and cheered.

Maria blushed. 'I don't know what came over me. It sort of just happened.'

'That's the actress in you,' said Patricia.

'What, the Neapolitan Pirate?' said Maria.

The table went quiet. Patricia looked down at her glass. Maria lifted Patricia's chin with her right arm and shook her head. 'It was a joke!'

Patricia wagged a finger. 'No, I deserved that, completely. I just want to say that I'm…'

'To Maria!' Charlie bellowed.

Glasses and cups were raised. They clinked together and everyone laughed when they spilt their drinks. The tourists walked past, pointing at the fountain, the dome of the Pantheon, the gelato shops and the horses. Nobody pointed at the group of friends at the table as they talked and laughed. Nobody recognised the English boy who had caused such a stir in the Campo de' Fiori. Why would they? He was just like any boy, really. Without his pictures and the legend of the *Charli Gatti*, he was nothing. A nobody. Just one of the gang. Charlie smiled. For the first time in his life, he was nothing. Just a boy with his friends, enjoying life and not worrying about what people thought about him and what he was going to be. He was living in the moment. It was a good moment.

Maria clicked her fingers and whistled. 'Snap out of it, Charlie. We've got to pay a visit to Signor

Roberto to pay him what we owe – oh, here's the money he owes your father for the sausage, Francisco…' She grabbed hold of Charlie's arm and pulled him up. 'Come on, we need to get your paints and canvas. You've got work to do!'

Charlie waved to the table gathering without looking and followed Maria to the art studio. Now was the real moment of truth: he simply had to win this exhibition, he just had to stay in Rome.

Charlie walked after the girl from the Via della Verita and thought about colliding stars. He was so lucky to have bumped into this one.

XXV

Bella sits looking up at the open window. The sound of music can be heard coming from the studio. Charlie is singing along.

'What a din,' says Adriana.

'I can't understand a word he's saying. It's just like *miao-miao-miao* or whatever,' says Bella.

'He's English,' says Bobby. 'Pretty much the same as *Americano*. He's singing the Rock 'n' Roll.'

'It just sounds like tomcats wailing,' says Bella.

'Anyway, what's it like to be famous *and* in love with Marco Del Vecchio?'

'Be quiet, Adriana! For the first time since I arrived here, I'm feeling that everything is going to be okay. But if you go around saying things like that, I'll be on the *Wanted* list again.'

'I think he's got a soft spot for you,' says Bobby.

'Who has got a soft spot?' says Angelina, jumping up onto the fountain.

'The English boy,' says Adriana quickly.

'Oh, him - I see. They're all talking about the *English Fella and Mozzarella Bella* after this morning. If cats ever needed a bit of "PR", now is the time. You've done well, Bella. I underestimated you. Do you think after everything that's happened, we can be friends?'

'Can *we* be friends, Angelina?' says Adriana.

'Well, that all depends on Bella here. Are we good?'

'We're all good, Angelina.'

'Then we're all friends together. But tell me, what is that noise?'

Bella nods at Charlie's balcony.

'Oh my, it's as well he doesn't paint as badly as he sings. Why is he making that racket? He sounds like he's in pain. Mind, he took a few big hits from Tito and Fino yesterday at the Forum. Go and take a look, Bella. Make sure he's okay; we don't want to lose such a fine asset to the business the moment we've found him.'

Bella takes her leave and makes her way up to Charlie's balcony.

What a mess! There are pieces of paper and paint pots everywhere. Is this the aftermath of her chasing after the rat this morning? But no, these are different pictures and rough sketches, and the paint pots are mostly empty. Charlie pops his head around the canvas he is stood behind. It looks like most of the paint is on his face.

'Bella! What are you doing here?'

Nope, still don't understand a word of what he says. Speak Italian, for God's sake! Hang on, I think he is. Yeah, that's it, speak VERY slowly, because I'm an idiot and your Italian is dreadful. What's that? You're painting a picture for an... exhibition in the Colosseum. Okay, got that. But what's it got to do with me? Now he's waving at me, crazy paint boy. What did you say? Pizza? Well, now you're talking my language.

Bella skips into the apartment and nibbles at the offering. Then she looks at the canvas.

Oh, my word!

'Now don't touch anything, Bella. More importantly, please don't tell anybody. It's a secret.'

'Charlie! Can I come up?'

It was Maria, calling up from outside his window.

'Yes!' he called out to the night.

Charlie put a finger to his lips. 'Especially not to her, do you hear me?'

Maria was banging at the door. 'What's keeping you? Let me in, please!'

Charlie opened the door and bowed. '*La mia casa è la tua casa.*'

Maria surveyed the wreckage and looked critically at Charlie's face. 'I see you've been busy… hello, what's she doing here?'

She? The cheek of it. What are you *doing here? And step away from the pizza, lady.*

Maria tiptoed across the room to avoid the mess and went to look at the canvas.

'No, Maria – you mustn't, please…'

Maria turned, abruptly. 'A blank canvas! What have you been doing all afternoon? I don't believe it, Charlie; all this scribbling on scraps of paper and splashing paint all over your face – wait a minute… if you've got paint all over your face, that means you've been painting. So how come the canvas is blank?'

'*Elementare, mia cara Maria.*'

'Don't you give me the *elementare*…'; and she ran up to him and jabbed him with her right wrist.

'Oh, no, not that again, please...'

'Tell me where the painting is.'

Another jab to the ribs.

'Okay, I give up. That tickles… Ouch, no – that hurts.'

Maria held her right wrist up to his face. 'Tell me, Charlie.'

'Signor Roberto. He came by to see how things were getting on. I had the idea all in my head. What time was it we left the others? Three or four o'clock? I'd finished by seven, and as I stepped onto the balcony for some fresh air, Signor Roberto walked by and asked if I'd finished. When I said yes, I had, well, then he wanted to come up and have a look. He saw the painting and offered to drive it straight over to the *Accademia*. Apparently, all the other entries were already in. Mine was the last. He took my entrance fee and the canvas, and I was just about to start on a new piece when Bella showed up. And then you came. Come on, help me tidy up and I'll buy you dinner. I've got some money left over.' Charlie jingled the loose change in his pockets.

Maria reached up and tidied a loose strand of hair behind his ear. It reminded him of when he first saw her working at *La Margherita*. 'What's wrong, Charlie? You look sad.'

'I was just thinking about what I'm going to do if I don't win the competition. I'll lose my place at the *Accademia* and have to go back to England. I mean, I've got enough money from the postcards to last about another week or so. But after that, what will I do?'

'You can start by switching on, Charlie,' said Maria, shaking his arm. 'Did we not sell one hundred sets of postcards today? We'll go out and sell some more tomorrow…'

'We can't tomorrow; I've got to help set things up at the Colosseum.'

'Next week, then. We can sell some more next week. I know the others will want to help.'

'No, Maria. I can't let you do that. Signor Roberto told me that your father's pizzeria has been allowed to open again. So, have all the other restaurants in the Via della Verita. You'll be needed more than ever now, and I can't ask Nico and Leonora to give up their spare time to help pay *my* way.'

'So, what if you don't win? What then, Charlie?'

'Then, I go back home to England.'

'I see. You go back home… to England.' She couldn't hide the disappointment in her voice.

'That was *always* going to happen, Maria. I was only supposed to be here for the summer. I got the crazy idea that I might be able to stay longer, but my mother hasn't answered my texts and the rent on this place runs out next week.'

'Yes. Of course. What was I thinking? Stupid kitten…'

'What was that?'

'Nothing, sorry. But you might still win, after all… maybe?' she said hopefully.

'Maybe, but there are a lot of good artists at the *Accademia*. Anyway, what about that dinner?'

'No, Charlie, not tonight. I'm sorry, I've got to help Papa get the restaurant ready for tomorrow. Big grand opening and all that.'

'Do you need a hand?'

'Another bad joke, Charlie?'

'I didn't mean anything by it…'

'So long, Charlie.'

Bella looked up from her pizza. This didn't look good. The canoodling couple - not so *canoodley*. The girl had just left, and the boy was walking out to the balcony. Bella trotted after him and they looked down into the street. Maria walked across the piazza and past the fountain. Charlie stood grasping the balcony rail. It was better this way. It was all moving too fast for him, anyway. Besides, this wasn't his home; he was a just another stranger in the Eternal City. He'd met some good friends and he'd have a few tales to tell back home. But that was it, really. Reality was so hard; it just reached up and slapped you in the face and brought you crashing back down to earth. Charlie watched another walking-train of tourists as it wormed its way in the direction of the Trevi fountain. Charlie's heart sank as he realised that, like the tourists, he didn't really belong here, either.

XXVI

Maria turned into Piazza Sant' Eustachio and walked straight up to the counter in the coffee shop and tapped Francisco on the shoulder.

'*Ciao*!' she waved at his face.

'*Buonasera…*,' said Francisco, and looked over his shoulder hesitantly.

'You okay?' asked Maria, who had been expecting to be kissed.

'Yes; it's just that I'm meeting somebody.'

'Patricia…' Maria wagged her finger. 'You guys will make a terrific couple. Or, are you meeting somebody else? Francisco, I didn't have you as the Casanova type,' she laughed. 'I'm shocked!'

Looking over Francisco's shoulder, Maria spotted him, even though he ducked into a doorway to try and avoid detection. She had never felt such loathing for anybody in her life. But what was he doing here meeting up with Francisco? Had he followed her?

She shook her head and patted Francisco's arm. 'I think your friend is here.' Maria walked away from the bar and stood tall in the doorway. Eventually, he turned, looked at her and strolled over to the coffee shop. How she despised his calm and cocky manner.

Maria spat on the floor at his feet. She would have spat in his ugly face, but he would probably have reported her to his old friends in the police on an assault charge.

Romano watched her walk off. Maria would pay for that display of insolence. They would all pay in the end, because ex-Police Chief Romano wasn't finished just yet.

Day 6

The Roman Forum – *Forum Romanum*

XXVII

The next morning the restaurant was closed. Charlie put his hands up to the window to shield his eyes and squinted into the dark interior. There were no tables and chairs outside on the pavement. It was gone nine o'clock; why were they not open for business? Charlie picked at the remains of the closure notice.

'You're too late. They've gone.' Amerigo walked across the street and set a chair down in his usual spot. 'Not bad, eh? I picked it up outside *The Black Rose*. I don't suppose they'll be needing it now,' he laughed.

'Gone where?' Charlie couldn't disguise the panic in his voice.

'So, you're bothered about her now, then? What happened to going back to England?'

'She told you?'

'Of course, she told me; she confides in me more than her own Papa. You fool…'

'I know. That's why I came around.'

'Well, that's just too bad; you're too late.' Amerigo snapped open his newspaper and began to read.

Charlie stepped forward and pulled the newspaper down. 'Amerigo, please, where have they gone?'

'Napoli.'

'Naples?'

'The very same. They left about five minutes ago – you've missed your chance. But then you probably knew that already.'

Charlie turned at the sound of a beeping horn. Nico was riding towards him, with Leonora waving frantically behind. As the scooter came to a halt, Leonora jumped off and pushed Charlie onto the vacated seat of the Lambretta. 'Go, go… idiot!'

Nico pulled away and looked over his shoulder. 'Idiot!'

Before Charlie had the chance to reply, they were racing along the cobbled street of the Via della Verita. The truth of the matter was that he was scared. Here he was, in a strange town, with no money, falling for a girl he hardly knew. In the circumstances, it was the best thing to do to let her down gently; and himself too. At least, that's what he thought yesterday evening. But then he'd dreamt again about his father's funeral and woke up in the early hours to the sound of Bella snoring in her orange crate. He stood on the balcony and looked out across Rome: a centuries-old vista. *Carpe Diem*: seize the day. Shakespeare again: *In delay there lies no plenty*. And whilst he was stood contemplating the uncertainty of the moment, a brown cat with white stockings jumped across from the neighbouring balcony. Without a second glance at Charlie, he walked into the apartment and settled in the orange crate next to Bella. *Be my guest*, thought Charlie.

Marco Del Vecchio didn't need any invitation.

Charlie had left the cats to munch on the leftover pizza from last night and wandered the streets. Did he really want to leave this place? He was young; who cares about the future? He was happy here.

Nico had taken every shortcut he knew in order to avoid the worst of the morning traffic as he weaved his way to Roma Termini train station. Pulling up outside, Nico pushed Charlie towards the entrance. 'The fast train is at twelve minutes past ten. Go! I'll wait here.'

'Thank you, Nico.' Charlie went to fist-bump.

Nico waved him away. 'No time for that. *Vai avanti!* Go!'

Charlie jogged through the station hall and looked up at the huge departures board. His eyes scrolled down the array of yellow letters, desperate to find the Naples train and the platform number: *Milano, Salerno, Pisa, Venezia…*

There, Napoli Centrale. Binario… Platform 3!

Charlie side-stepped and shuffled, dodged and bumped, and finally he was running along Platform 3, looking into the train windows, frantically searching for Maria and Toni. The train left in less than a minute, but it was surprisingly empty. Charlie jumped on the train and walked along the central aisle of the carriage. *Come on, where are they?* Charlie crouched down and looked along the entire length of the carriage. Nobody. Where were all the passengers? A guard's whistle and a dull thudding sound caused him to look out of the window at an adjacent train.

'Maria!'

She was banging on the window of her train.

They began to mime at each other through the glass, just as Maria's train started to pull away.

Maria: *What are you doing?*

Charlie: 'I came to see you.'

Maria: *What for?*

Charlie: 'Because…'

Charlie started to walk faster along the carriage. In order to see Maria, he had to duck his head down. He resorted to making hand signals.

Charlie pointed to his chest.

Maria nodded.

Charlie pointed down.

Maria shook her head.

Charlie pointed down again with both hands: 'Here!'

Maria nodded.

Charlie pointed at Maria.

Maria pointed to herself: *Mia?*

Charlie nodded: 'Yes, you!'

Maria pulled her mouth down and raised her palm, the classic Italian gesture: *What about me?*

Maria's train was moving faster.

Charlie was jogging now.

He pointed to his chest.

Then he pressed his thumbs and forefingers into a heart-shape.

And then he repeatedly jabbed his two forefingers at Maria: 'Yes, You, you, you!'

Then she was gone.

XXVIII

The Colosseum looked magnificent in the fading sun. Time turned to stone. The imposing edifice swallowed him up. Charlie greeted his fellow artists with great dignity and many cheek kisses as he walked into the exhibition hall. The hall had been set up on one of the upper floors of the old arena, and the display walls contained images of the students at work and newspaper clippings of previous winners. The students talked excitedly. Most dismissed their chances with a wave of the hand. Others joked about what they would do with the money. Charlie looked at the winners' stands. The chosen finalists – be they sculptures, ceramics, photography or paintings – were hidden from view. The sculpture stand looked particularly ghoulish, with the figures draped in white sheets. The painters' works were masked by newspaper. All the entries had to be the same size as the others in their discipline: the ceramic plates, the photographs, the statues, and the canvasses, all had to be submitted to strict specifications. That way, you couldn't tell if your piece had been chosen.

'Ladies and gentlemen, welcome to the fifteenth Art Exhibition hosted by the *Accademia Delle Belle Arti di Roma*.' Signora Raggi, the principal at the *Accademia*, had taken to the stage to address the assembled artists, judges and celebrity audience. 'It gives me great pleasure to welcome you all here today. I would like to start off by congratulating all of our entrants. The standard of work this year has been exceptionally high, and you all deserve a round of applause for your efforts...'

Signora Raggi clapped along with the audience.

'Now, I would also like to say to the entrants that the way this exhibition is run will serve you well in your professional lives. Not everybody can be a winner. That is a fact of life. You will find many doors slammed in your face along the way. Take life's disappointments as your inspiration. When you walk into the hall behind you, do not allow the disappointment of seeing your work on display affect your enjoyment of this evening. If your work is on display, it means you are not one of the finalists. But you should take pride in the fact you have entered the competition. You are all winners.'

Signora Raggi listened to the stifled clapping. Nerves were kicking in.

'The judges have picked the top three entries in each discipline, and they are here waiting to be unveiled. But before that we will go through to the other hall and enjoy the magnificence of the other entries. First, though, I would like to introduce to you our special guest. All the way from the Guggenheim Museum in New York, Mr Jerry Eisner…'

Charlie clapped along with the others and then stared at the stage. He looked to the wings and saw the woman without her floppy hat; her son was wearing his father's outsized *Let's Go Mets* baseball cap. Charlie's sketches had been bought by the curator of the Guggenheim Museum in New York! Charlie's head was reeling, and his heart thumped as he looked at the three paintings hidden beneath the faded copies of *Il Messaggero*. As they wandered into the other hall, Charlie was standing up on tip-toe, trying to catch sight of the canvasses that had been hung along the far wall. The photography entrants were on the left, watercolours to his right. The sculptures and ceramics were laid out in the centre. Charlie bumped into Patricia.

'How did you do?' he asked.

'I can't find my photo, so I'm presuming that I've made the top three.' Patricia bobbed on her toes.

'Well done!' Charlie kissed her cheek.

'What about you?'

'I don't know.'

'Come, let's go see…' Patricia took Charlie's hand and led him to the far wall.

He scanned the canvasses and shook his head. 'No, it's not here.' He checked again. His canvas was absent from the display of works.

Patricia gave Charlie a hug. 'You did it! Come on, let's mix.'

'You go. I just want to check out the competition.' Charlie pointed to the wall. He wanted to double-check his painting was not there.

There was no doubt that he had done really well to get into the final. The other students' work was amazing. But Charlie knew his picture was good. It was very good, and that wasn't him being conceited. Charlie had told a story in his picture – a simple story of yesterday and today, captured in a single moment of time throughout the ages. He calmly shook hands with the other artists and asked them about the inspiration behind their work. *Listen to other people*, his father would tell him; it was one of the key essentials in how to win friends and influence people. Perhaps that was why his father was so good with women? Charlie listened to the students and praised their efforts. The sound of a gong signalled that it was time for the final to take place.

The art exhibition was judged by leading academics and the trustees of the *Accademia* –

including Signor Roberto. It was this group who determined the final three pieces for each discipline. The final phase was an auction contested by the top three entries in each discipline, explained Patricia.

'The *Accademia* produces a catalogue on the eve of the exhibition and invites bids for all the pieces. No actual money is exchanged at this stage; it's just an estimation of what the academics, trustees or dignified guests might be willing to pay on the open market. The works that attract the highest total of bids make it through to the final three. The assembled dignitaries will now be able to bid proper for each piece. The work that attracts the highest bid wins. You're going to have to wait until the end – they always do the paintings last of all.'

Charlie watched the events unfold. The ceramic pieces started off at two hundred euros each. The auctioneer inviting bids for each of the works in turn. At two hundred and eighty euros, the first piece, a jug, was eliminated, having been sold to a Contessa Ravelli. The final items were a plate and a vase. The bids edged up past three hundred euros and the audience got more animated. At three hundred and forty-two euros, the plate was sold to Mr Hampson-Smith, from England.

'What happens now?' asked Charlie, momentarily distracted at hearing the name:

Hampson-Smith. Wasn't that the name of the Eisner's friends in London?

'There appear to be two buyers interested in the vase, so the auction continues. If there was only one bidder, then he would get it for whatever the last piece went for, plus one euro.' Patricia was an informative guide.

The vase attracted more bids. The auctioneer was rattling through the prices and the nods and fingers kept signalling their interest. Until…

Four hundred and twenty-one euros: going once, going twice – SOLD! To Mr Jerry Eisner, of the Guggenheim Museum of New York.

'Is he allowed to bid again?' asked Charlie. He looked around, but Patricia had gone.

But then he heard her voice.

'Of course; he can come back to the bidding any time he likes. He could buy all the pieces if he really wanted to…'

Charlie felt the electricity of her touch and shut his eyes to capture the moment forever. This was something he had never experienced before. It was all a bit grown up, really. But the touch of her hand and the stellar blue of her eyes completely bedazzled him.

'I've decided not to go away just yet.' Charlie turned to Maria. 'I think I might hang around for a bit, you know? See the sites, visit a few museums.

Sell a few postcards… I thought you'd gone back to Naples?'

'We did, so Papa could order a new clay pizza oven. The restaurant re-opening has given him a new lease of life. He's going to completely refurbish the place, and he's ordered a new coffee machine, too. He's very old fashioned and likes to do business face-to-face. So, we went down to Naples. It gave him a chance to catch up with his sister. It only takes just over an hour to get to Naples on the fast train, Charlie. You'd jumped on the slow one. Anyway, what was it you were trying to say to me through the window?'

Next up, ladies and gentlemen, we have the finalists in the photography class…

'Look, there's Patricia – she's in the final three.' Charlie walked over to Patricia, who was gnawing at her fingers in anticipation. Maria kept trying to ask him what it was that he was saying to her on the train, but he either ignored her or deflected the question. The bidding for the photographs got to just over one hundred euros, and Patricia's work was sold first. An honourable third; she hadn't expected to get in the final and was ecstatic.

'What does this mean?' Maria asked Patricia, holding up her left hand with the forefinger crooked and thumb extended.

Patricia mirrored the movement, holding her right hand up to Maria's. '*Amore*. The heart sign. *Amor e Roma*. Love is Rome and Rome is Love. Why?'

Charlie said, 'Come on, guys…'

Patricia formed her fingers into the heart sign and then pointed at Charlie.

Maria giggled.

Finally, ladies and gentlemen, we come to the last auction: the painting class; and here are the finalists…

With great ceremony, the newspaper was ripped from each of the three canvasses. Charlie's painting was in the middle. It wouldn't have mattered if there was a Caravaggio or a Raphael either side of Charlie's painting – Maria wouldn't have taken any notice of them. Her eyes were drawn to the woman in Charlie's painting. The woman was running right out of the painting and straight towards her. She wore a royal blue shift dress and her face was tilted up to the sun. You could feel the warmth of her smile as it radiated from the canvas, and you wanted to reach out and touch her long, brown hair as it fell about her shoulders. The woman was running towards Maria. In her left hand, which was raised above her head, she held a silk scarf that unfurled like a flag behind her. The scarf was coloured navy blue and yellow, with little cats drawn in the pattern. It was exactly like the scarf her Papa had bought for Mamma in London. Maria turned to Charlie with tears in her eyes.

Mamma. You painted Mamma.

Charlie had captured the inner beauty of Valeria Viola without ever having set eyes on her. He had to work from the memory of the images of her in the media clippings and studio portraits that adorned the walls of *La Margherita*. Maria wanted to reach out and touch the canvas. But as she stepped forward, she looked closer. Mamma was running through the Roman Forum, and behind her in the distance was a clutter of cats making a nuisance of themselves around a gattara. Imprinted on the crumbling columns were images of gladiators and lions, and the graffiti on the wall read: *Roma e Amor*. Old and new. Rome and love.

'Incredible, isn't it?' The man spoke with an American accent. 'My wife cried when she saw it, too.' The man pointed to a woman who was holding the hand of a little boy wearing a baseball cap, and then offered a tissue.

Maria wiped the tears from her face.

The man pointed to Charlie's painting. 'I take it this is your mother?'

May I have opening bids of three hundred euros? Yes, thank you, Sir. Madam – over there, yes? Sir. Madam. On the telephone...

The first painting went for three hundred and fifty euros.

The second for three hundred and sixty-five…

The next round of bidding for Charlie's painting started at four hundred euros. Charlie had won, but he was so caught up with the excitement of the auction that it didn't register. How much would somebody be willing to pay for his painting?

'The *Accademia* takes ten percent. The rest is all yours,' whispered Patricia.

Four hundred euros to my left… Four-twenty…

Charlie tried to see who was bidding for his painting, but the movements were in the shadows. He tried to read the faces and body language, but he couldn't see who was pushing the price up higher and yet higher.

Four hundred and fifty euros – five hundred? Five hundred it is on the telephone. Who will give me five-fifty? Six hundred, Madam…

So dumbstruck was he with the proceedings that it was only now that Charlie realised the auction was being conducted in English. Was he really going to have his art displayed in the Guggenheim Museum? That had to be the reason why the auction was in English – so Mr Eisner could bid for his painting.

'What's happening, Charlie? My English isn't that good – he says the numbers so quickly. I don't know why they insist on doing the auction in English every year.'

So that was the reason. Charlie chastised himself for his being so arrogant as to think it was all about his painting and Mr Eisner.

Seven hundred euros, seven hundred and ten… Madam? Seven hundred and fifteen, thank you. Any more at seven hundred and fifteen? Who will give me seven hundred and twenty? No? Seven hundred and sixteen? Thank you, Sir. Seventeen? Madam.

The numbers were getting closer, which meant that the bidders were reaching the point of no return. Charlie's painting was going to be sold for over seven hundred euros.

Going once. Going twice… Once more… at seven hundred and twenty euros… SOLD!

The gavel came crashing down and the audience clapped as one. It was a record price for an *Accademia* auction, and Charlie was swamped by his classmates and peers. He shook hands, kissed cheeks, nodded thanks and smiled. England was on hold, for the moment. Time to live in the here and now, although he would have to find a cheaper apartment.

'Congratulations, young man. I reckon I've got myself a sound investment.'

Charlie shook the American's hand. 'Mr Eisner, what can I say? Thank you for buying my painting.'

'Your painting?' Jerry Eisner puffed out his cheeks. 'I was talking about your sketches. And I got a pack of those postcards, too. I was wrong about signing yourself off as Charles, by the way. *Charli Gatti* has a ring to it. No, I didn't get your painting. I was outbid; now I've got to figure out how to explain to my wife that I couldn't bid any higher because she'd spent too much money on that damned vase. But that's my problem. Your problem is you don't realise how talented you are. That painting is awesome. Valeria Viola and *The Lions of Rome*. I remember that film. I'm a great lover of her movies. You've used *that* image to good effect. Well, good evening, young man, and be sure to look me up when you're in New York. Here's my card.'

Charlie took the business card. 'Thank you, Sir.'

Now he was confused. Who had won the auction? Who had out-bid Jerry Eisner? But now the halls emptied. The auctioneer packed away his gavel and catalogue. Signora Raggi exited with the dignitaries. Jerry Eisner and his wife left with their son, who reached out and waved at Charlie. The students all agreed to meet up in the latest trendy bar in Trastevere. The security staff stepped outside for a cigarette break.

Charlie and Maria were alone.

'You have a great talent,' said Maria.

'I can but try. Thank you for everything. I'm sorry about last night…'

'It's a great painting. You really captured her. It's an amazing likeness. How did you manage to get her just so perfect? And when did you learn about *The Lions of Rome*? It was Mamma's last film.'

Charlie looked up at the canvas. 'It was easy, really. I just had to look into your eyes.'

'Ah, *but love looks not with the eyes but with the mind*. Isn't that what Shakespeare says, English? I must say that you have captured her magnificently.' Romano held his hands behind his back and admired Charlie's painting. 'It will look good on my wall. You know how much of a fan I am of your mother, Maria.'

'You bid for the painting?' Maria felt her arms being held and, turning her head, she saw the grinning face of Tito.

'What's happening?' Charlie struggled against the vice-like grip of Fino.

'You've already met my nephews.' Romano spoke in English. 'A pair of ignorant oafs they may be, but they have their uses.'

'*You* bought my painting?'

'Don't flatter yourself, English. Where would I get seven hundred and twenty euros from? I mean, I'm no longer employed by the Rome City Police, and my little business venture has gone bust. You may have heard that there was an unfortunate incident – an awful mess in the Piazza del Paradiso? The Comandante in his wisdom has seen fit to suspend me from duty. Some people may think this is a reason to be cheerful, or an excuse to spit at me…'

'I didn't spit at you, I spat at your feet. I should have spat in your face, though – you pig!'

Charlie was taken aback by Maria's anger. That would be the Neapolitan in her. *Note to self: Do NOT upset this girl.*

Romano held up his hands. 'I get it. You hate me. I would probably hate me, too, if I wasn't me. But I am me, and I'm rather fond of me, and now I'm going to take possession of this rather lovely painting.' Romano stepped up onto the stand and lifted the canvas from the wall.

'Stop, thief!' shouted Maria.

Romano laughed in Maria's face.

Tito and Fino laughed.

'No-one can hear you,' whispered Tito, his rank breath laced with menace.

'I'll get security,' said Maria.

'Tut-tut, didn't you recognise Francisco? He's in charge around here. It pays to know the right people,' said Romano, wrapping the canvas in newspaper and heading for the exit.

'But what are you going to do with the painting? I mean, what use is it to you?' screamed Charlie. No matter how hard he struggled, he couldn't break free from Fino's grasp. The boy was strong.

'Here's the scenario: the painting goes missing, the bidder then refuses to part with any cash and the student-boy here has to go back to merry England.'

'What is it with you?' said Maria. 'It's the stupidest plan I ever heard. You're just mean and completely deluded.'

'What is it with me? I'll tell you what it is, Maria. I just can't stand to see other people happy, that's all. I was happy once, when I was working at *La Margherita* and I saw your mother every single blessed day. I fell in love with her back then, and I'm still in love with her now. But she was in love with your father, and you don't know how much it hurts me to see people *really* happy.'

'You're sick.'

'Maybe I am – sick with love. But now she is no longer here, rest her soul. So, what have I got to live for, other than to make you and your father as miserable as me, and if that means ensuring this boy gets on the next flight back to England, then so be it!'

'You are just plain sick.' Charlie stamped down hard on Fino's foot, causing him to release his grip, and rushed towards his brother, who still held Maria.

Tito pulled Maria to one side. 'Don't come any closer or I'll slit her throat.'

Charlie looked at the knife that Tito held against Maria's neck.

Maria was shaking uncontrollably.

She was scared.

Charlie was scared.

Tito was as mad as his uncle. There was no telling what he would do. But, at the very moment that Charlie was juggling with his thoughts, Francisco came screaming through the hall, chased by dozens of cats. Romano watched open-mouthed as the butcher's son frantically sought sanctuary. These cats were angry, and they meant business.

Hiss!

Romano looked up.

From the shadows of the great Colosseum, the cats emerged.

Hundreds of them.

'Good God! What is all this nonsense?'

The cats jumped down into the exhibition hall and, as they did so, others came running in from the open doorways. Some ran towards Romano, who dropped the canvas to the floor and jumped up onto one of the stands. Others rushed at Fino, who ran in the direction of the outer hall and was knocked down by the hapless Francisco as he desperately tried to escape his pursuers. Then the gang, led by Marco Del Vecchio, turned their attention towards Tito.

'I'm warning you, kitties – stay back or the girl gets it!'

Bella jumped.

The tortoiseshell had stolen up onto one of the metal girders that supported the Colosseum arches. She had looked down and seen the glint of the knife. The boy holding it was one of the two brothers who had stoned Franco. Marco had given her the full rundown of the events in the Roman Forum, and Bella's thirst for revenge was insatiable. She sat back on her haunches and waited for the moment to pounce. One slip and the girl could die. Bella had to get her timing spot on. The other brother crashing into the security guard was the signal. Tito, for a fraction of a second, relinquished his grip on Maria. One second was all that Bella needed.

Bella jumped.

Tito screamed as Bella dug her claws into the back of his neck.

Maria fell to the floor.

The cats' howls echoed around the Colosseum: a cacophony of screams and wails that was enough to wake the dead. Romano held his hands to his ears and shook his head feverishly.

The din was only silenced by the echo of a gunshot.

Charlie dived on top of Maria.

Police!

Stop there!

Don't move!

'I'm sure that firing bullets into World Heritage sites is an imprisonable offence, Officer Raphael, but I might be inclined to turn a blind eye in the circumstances. Arrest Romano and his good-for-nothing nephews!' bellowed the Comandante.

The hall was suddenly full of Rome City Police and Carabinieri officers.

Charlie picked Maria up off the floor.

'Are you okay, young man?' asked the Comandante.

'Mozzarella Bella saved Maria,' said Charlie. 'I wouldn't have believed it if I hadn't seen it with my own eyes, but I think all the cats came here deliberately to get Romano. They were organised and knew exactly what they were doing and exactly *who* they were after. I'm serious. It was incredible.'

The Comandante looked over his shoulder to ensure that nobody was close enough to hear, and whispered into Charlie's ear, 'If I hadn't witnessed them rush into *The Black Rose* restaurant in Piazza del Paradiso yesterday, I would say you were completely mad - *pazzo*. But I'm inclined to agree with your observations. However, for the moment it might be wise to keep these thoughts to ourselves.'

Charlie nodded.

'Now, to business. Officer Raphael, fetch me those two over there.'

Raphael pushed Tito and Fino in front of the Comandante.

'You are both under arrest on suspicion of cruelty and causing unnecessary suffering to animals, and robbery.' The Comandante turned to Charlie. 'I take it that you still wish to press charges?'

'What evidence do you have?' cried Tito.

'Yes, what evidence have you got?' Fino chipped in for good measure.

The Comandante held out his hand to Officer Raphael and took the sheet of paper that was held together by dozens of strips of clear tape. 'The likeness is uncanny. Are these your sketches of the two people that you say attacked you in the Roman Forum, Signor Charlie?'

Charlie inspected the paper. It had been torn to tiny shreds and then pieced together like a jigsaw puzzle. 'Yes, I can confirm this is the sketch that I drew and handed to Officer Raphael at the police station.'

'Good! Take them away, please. You, young man, are not fit to wear that AS Roma shirt – you're a disgrace to the *Giallorossi*. No, Officer Raphael – not you – stay where you are, please. I need you to explain to *ex*-Police Chief Romano how this evidence came into your possession.'

Officer Raphael coughed to clear his throat. 'Signor Charlie drew the sketches for me when I was station duty officer at the time of making his complaint of robbery. The witness told me that he had been attacked whilst trying to intervene in saving a cat from being stoned in the Roman Forum. He had injuries to his face and hands and two hundred euros had been stolen from his person.'

'What has this got to do with me?' implored Romano. 'I can't be held responsible for the actions of my nephews – I wasn't there. What evidence have you got to implicate me?'

'No, Sir – you were not there in the Forum. But you came into the police station when the matter was being reported by Signor Charlie and you took this sketch of the suspects from him. I think you said you were going to take *personal charge* of the investigation?'

'And I did say that. I am determined to get to the bottom of this despicable act.' Romano turned to the Comandante. 'Trust me, sir. Family or not, this was a dreadful attack on an innocent boy and a poor defenceless animal.'

'Then kindly explain how the drawing ended up torn to pieces in your waste bin – *Sir*?' Raphael then showed Romano a still from the CCTV footage that showed him outside the police station ripping the page in half.

The Comandante spoke directly into Romano's face: 'You are under arrest on suspicion of two counts of misconduct in a public office. One: you have wilfully tried to cover up a crime. Two: You have been involved in an unregistered business interest with your involvement in *The Black Rose* restaurant and abused your position of trust by closing down your competitors with false claims of breaches of a long-forgotten by-law...'

'But a by-law, nevertheless, Comandante...'

'Shut up, Romano! You have abused your position as a police officer to bring misery to many business owners in the Via della Verita – now, isn't that the truth?'

'Comandante, I'm afraid that these crimes that you speak of are nothing compared to what I have to tell you.' The dark figure of the Gattara emerged from behind one of the columns. She walked with purpose towards the centre of the hall and pointed at Romano. 'I witnessed this man murder Valeria

Viola. I saw him drive his car at her deliberately as she cycled away from his apartment. She didn't stand a chance.'

Romano turned to the Comandante. 'Are you going to take the word of a simple Gattara? What is she talking about? This is an outrageous lie. A defamation of character. This woman is crazy...'

The Gattara untied the black scarf she wore on her head and uncovered her face.

Charlie and Maria looked at each other with wide eyes. They had expected to see the wizened face of an old woman. What they saw was a fine-boned woman of some fifty years, with grey hair that was bobbed to her shoulders.

'Contessa Ravelli?'

'Good evening, Comandante.'

Maria gasped.

The woman let her tattered outer garments fall to the floor; underneath she was wearing a stylish trouser suit and sported a navy, yellow and black silk scarf. A scarf with cats etched into the pattern. The Contessa took off the scarf and walked over to Maria. She placed the scarf around Maria's neck and kissed her on both cheeks. 'Maria, I was an old friend of your late mother.' The Contessa held up her hand to prevent Maria from speaking. 'I know what you're thinking – *who is this woman*? We have never met, and I haven't seen your father in over twenty years. You see, I was the understudy to your mother when she was an actress. I did all her stunts and stood in for her on the longshots when she was busy filming the important scenes. When the studio sacked your mother, they promoted me in her place. What could I do? I was young, I was ambitious. But I didn't have her talent. It wasn't long before the studio dumped me, too. Then I married a wonderful and very wealthy man and lost touch with your parents. One day, about two years ago, I bumped into your mother when I was out shopping, and we exchanged contact details. We would meet up occasionally for dinner, but she wouldn't tell your father for fear of upsetting him, as he hated to be reminded of how the studio had treated her so badly. And then there was this dreadful business with the car and her bicycle…' The Contessa took a deep breath and appeared lost in her thoughts as she gazed upon Maria's innocent face.

'Contessa, you were saying about an incident with the car and a bicycle…,' prompted the Comandante.

'Incident, Comandante? It was murder, plain and simple. It was an awful night. The rain was pouring down and the streets were flooded. I saw Valeria cycling along, and this car – a white Fiat 500 – came hurtling up behind her and…'

'This is nonsense. Where is the proof? Where is this car – this white Fiat 500?' demanded Romano.

'Proof? Well, Comandante, you see this scarf' – the Contessa toyed with the ends of the scarf she had placed around Maria's neck – 'I just happened to come across this scarf quite by chance a few days ago. I do not sleep very well and tend to walk the streets in the early hours. Anyway, I saw a cat run out of a lock-up in the Piazza del Paradiso and the cat had this very scarf wrapped around her legs and neck. You will remember seeing me, no doubt, Romano?'

Romano shrugged. 'How would I have seen you? I wasn't there. This is nonsense.'

'Forgive me, Romano. You are correct – you didn't see me at all. You saw a simple gattara, for I have walked these streets dressed as such for this past year. After what I witnessed that night with Valeria, I was determined to get the proof to ensure you paid for what you did. I saw you driving that Fiat 500. I saw you kill Valeria!'

'But why did you not just come straight to the police at the time, Contessa?' asked the Comandante.

'You will forgive me for saying this, Comandante, but I was afraid I wouldn't be believed. Who would believe my word against that

243

of Romano, a respected Police Chief? All he would have to say was that he didn't see her – that the weather and road conditions made driving difficult... I'm afraid that I didn't have faith in the police or the criminal justice system. I apologise for that now, Comandante. However, I decided to gather more evidence and make it impossible for Romano to find any wiggle room. So, I walked the streets dressed as the Gattara and watched and waited. It was pure chance that I saw Bella come running out of the lock-up with the scarf wrapped around her legs... and here she is – how are you, sweetie?' The Contessa tickled Bella under the chin. 'If you go to the lock-up in the Pizza del Paradiso, you will find the car, Comandante. The front end has much damage, and there is the red paint from Valeria's bicycle on the bumper...'

Maria couldn't hold herself back any longer. 'And Mamma's scarf was never found at the time. She must have left it at your apartment that night when she came to see you – to warn you off for good. You murderer! You cold-hearted murderer!'

Charlie caught her and held her tight in his arms. He felt her body shake as sobs wracked her whole being. Maria's hurt and anger caused Charlie to shiver uncontrollably.

'Officer Raphael – take him away!' The Comandante signalled to his men that it was time for them to go. 'Contessa, I will send someone round to see you in the morning for your statement. Thank you.' The Comandante gave Maria a consoling pat on the shoulder. Bella mewed. 'It's funny,' he said to the Contessa, 'but if I didn't know better, I would swear this cat could talk.'

The Contessa smiled. 'She can. And she said: *thank you.*'

The Comandante raised a finger to his hat in salute to the tortoiseshell cat and walked briskly out of the hall.

'Now, let's take another look at my painting…' The Contessa picked up Charlie's canvas from the floor and held it up in front of her as she walked to the exhibition stand. Once she had squarely fixed the canvas back on the wall, she stepped back. 'I hope you spend the money wisely, young man. I take it that the money will pay for food and keep? You needn't worry about lodgings, as I have plenty of rooms. If you don't mind cats, that is… You'll be pleased to know that the little fellow whose rescue you came to in the Roman Forum is making a good recovery… Yes, Bella – Franco is going to be okay. He's still very sore – but he will live.'

Bella mewed.

Charlie and Maria stared at the Contessa.

'You bid for Charlie's painting?' said Maria.

The Contessa dabbed at Maria's tears with the ends of the scarf. 'Yes, dear. I fell in love with it as soon as I saw it in the catalogue – which was incredibly late in being despatched this year; in fact, I only received a copy late last night – and even though they don't give the name of the artist, I knew who had painted this little masterpiece. I've been a trustee of the *Accademia* since I retired from acting. You know, Charlie, I think you've captured her perfectly…'

'As soon as the painting was unveiled, I recognised Mamma. It wasn't just the scarf, it was everything: her face, her smile, her eyes…,' said Maria.

'Maria, come here, please.' The Contessa stood behind Maria and placed her hands on her shoulders. 'Now, look again – closely – and tell me who you really see.'

Maria studied the painting up close. She touched the scarf she was wearing and held a finger to the canvas, tracing the contours of the billowing silk that trailed behind the beautiful and familiar image. 'It *is* Mamma; Charlie has really captured her timeless beauty…'

'Look again, Maria,' interrupted the Contessa. 'There, now you see it. Charlie hasn't painted your mother – he's painted you.'

Maria stared.

It was like looking at a mirror image. For, whilst the clothing suggested that the woman was Valeria Viola, the detail of the right hand told another story. Maria leaned into the canvas. At first glance the viewer would think that the right hand of the figure was being held behind her back. But no, there was a definite gap. It was subtle and deceptive. You were so drawn to the radiant beauty of the central figure that you didn't notice that she had a hand missing. The English student had taken an iconic image of Valeria Viola and turned it into his own timeless masterpiece... of Maria.

Maria turned and walked over to Charlie, who was sat canoodling with Bella:

'O mistress mine, where are you roaming? O stay and hear! Your true-love's coming.'

Maria knelt down and put her arms around Charlie's neck. Then she kissed him.

Day 7

The Colosseum – *Il Colosseo*

XXIX

I hear her singing as she crosses the Via della Verita:
I'm walking pretty
Through the streets of the Eternal City
Wherever I roam, every street's my home
When I'm roaming in Rome.

I say, 'Well, look who it is? Mozzarella Bella. And where have you been roaming this fine morning?'

Bella says: 'Here and there, and everywhere.'

They're all here: Toni and the Contessa sit talking with Amerigo; Nico sits behind Leonora and cuddles her as she pretends to drive his scooter. Patricia talks animatedly with Maria – she's over the Francisco thing. And, of course, there's Charlie, who brought us all back together, really. And then you've got Angelina, Bobby, Adriana, and Franco, who is almost back to full fitness and still as grumpy as ever.

Imagine this.

Maria tucks a loose strand of hair behind her ear and calls to Charlie: '*Un cappuccino, un espresso e la pizza margherita*! Coffees and pizza;

and make it snappy!' She tidies the *Charli Gatti* postcards in the stand and looks down the street. The tourists are flocking back to the Via della Verita. The restaurants and bars are open, and the place is buzzing again. You know what they call this place? They call it the *Naples Quarter* – where you can buy the best pizzas in Rome.

Amerigo says, 'I see that brute Romano has got ten years, the fascist pig!'

Patricia says, 'Let me take a picture of you, Amerigo. Come on, put your newspaper down and say *cheese* for the camera!' She clicks the button and Amerigo grins a toothless smile.

Charlie pokes his head through the bug blinds. 'Did you say pizza? I've never made a pizza before. I'm only the barista, remember?'

Amerigo says, 'A barista – really? I've tasted your coffee, Charlie. Are you sure you've made that before?'

Toni laughs. 'No time like the present to learn the trade of the *pizzaiolo*.'

'A *pizza-whato*?'

'A pizza-maker. Never mind. Come on, the Mozzarella Bella and her gang are hungry!' and Toni pushes Charlie back inside the restaurant.

Maria says, 'How's Charlie settling in, Contessa?'

The Contessa says, 'His room is a pig-sty. What a mess! But his paintings are so very good, so we can forgive him this one fault. Are you glad he decided to stay?'

Maria nods.

The Contessa smiles and reaches up to tuck a loose strand of hair behind Maria's ear and murmurs, *Che bella* – beautiful.

Nico and Leonora are now a canoodling couple. *Roma e Amore.*

Rome is love.

I like the canoodling couples - all of them. Who knows what'll happen to them in time? Unlike me, they only get the one chance at this life. For now, they are living in the very moment in the timelessness of the Eternal City. Where better place in the world to be?

Another day in Rome.

Except you know, by now, that there is no such thing – right?

So, there you have it: the story of the *Mozzarella Bella and the English Fella.*

Who am I?

Why, my name is Marco Del Vecchio. Me and my boys look after all the business right here in the Via della Verita. One day I might tell you *my* story.

Arrivederci!

CPSIA information can be obtained
at www.ICGtesting.com
Printed in the USA
LVHW031736030619
619985LV00003B/671/P